THE HOUSE OF MADELAINE

THE HOUSE
OF MADELAINE

A NOVEL

ELAINE KRAF

Introduction by Jamie Hood

THE MODERN LIBRARY

NEW YORK

The Modern Library
An imprint of Random House
A division of Penguin Random House LLC
1745 Broadway, New York, NY 10019
modernlibrary.com
randomhousebooks.com
penguinrandomhouse.com

2024 Modern Library Edition

First published by Doubleday & Company, Inc. in 1971.

Paperback ISBN 978-0-593-73188-8
Ebook ISBN 978-0-593-73187-1

Printed in the United States of America on acid-free paper

1st Printing

The authorized representative in the EU for product safety and compliance is Penguin Random House Ireland, Morrison Chambers, 32 Nassau Street, Dublin D02 YH68, Ireland. https://eu-contact.penguin.ie

IN MEMORY OF DONNA KEATH

INTRODUCTION
JAMIE HOOD

Elaine Kraf's second novel, *The House of Madelaine*, was published by Doubleday in 1971, two years after her debut, *I Am Clarence*, at the dawn of a decade defined by "women's lib," or what is now more commonly called feminism's "Second Wave." The novel opens as many fairy tales do: Two women journey "through a long aisle of dark bushes" toward a mysterious house "whose existence was confirmed by a wooden door [with] no place for a key." The fate awaiting them is what awaits countless girls in such fables—the love of a man. Romance! The marriage plot! Happily ever after? And so on.

Elaine, our heroine, is a former kindergarten teacher at "P.S. X." (Kraf worked as a special education teacher and school principal.) She joins her friend Florence in search of Florence's lover, Gerard, who is hidden away in the house among a small coterie of totemic side characters: the Lady Poet Hannah; Hannah's paternalistic partner Alfred; Florence's dreamy brother Joseph; their mother; and their father, the gibberish-spewing Sir Phalatrope, Elaine's lone ally in the house. There is also, yes, the titular Madelaine, the house's architect and puppet master, who seems to see, know, and manipulate all that transpires within its walls.

Once the women are suspended inside, days unspool feverishly, and they lose track of the lives they'd lived before. Hitherto-unseen rooms and whole floors materialize without explanation; characters dissolve, disappear, or die only to return a half-dozen pages later, proving previous events utterly immaterial. It's an absurdist's fantasy—an example, perhaps, of what some scholars have named the "literary nonsense genre"—severed from time, identity, and reason, and brimming over with spectral mothers, dark doubles, enigmatic white horses, and perverted wax men. Inexplicable signs and symbols shade in the edges of scenes, which are witnessed as if from behind the veil of Madelaine's black taffeta slips. I can't help but think David Lynch would have had a field day with it.

When she catches Elaine documenting her experiences in a notebook, Madelaine tells her that her "words are refuse—a collage of floral embroidery. There is no character analysis or plot." It's an arrestingly meta-textual exchange, like spying through a keyhole on an artist mercilessly reflecting on her own process. Trauma disjoints conventional narrative; Elaine's diary-keeping might illuminate something about the desire to wrestle chaos into recognizability through writing. Formally speaking, the novel is flitting and hybrid, a kind of textual patchwork: Its dreamscapes dance between plainspoken and baroque prose, yes, but also poetry, musical notation, and sequences that read like experimental theater or procedural television.

Still, the story has recognizable beats. Madelaine orchestrates nightly dinners to tug the house's wandering misfits back into orbit. Elaine falls in love with Joseph, who arrives as a visual composite of her romantic longings—and who reminds her of a shadowy husband-figure in her increasingly opaque past—but who soon compels Elaine to slough off her delusions of love and engage in sex work in a sort of underground bunker illuminated by red lights. In the back half of the novel, Elaine is put on trial: first, on charges against her right to claim poetic authorship, and second, for Alfred's murder (who, in one example of apparent resurrection, himself acts as the trial's district attorney).

If the particulars blur and baffle, the soul of the novel sings through: Rather than a tale of lost love found, *The House of Mad-*

elaine is the story of a woman who is being stripped of her identity, who no longer seems to know what it is she wants or who she might yet become. Lewis Carroll's Alice seems an obvious influence for Elaine, with the world of the house a kind of Wonderland, a topsy-turvy refraction of the outside. While the house defies the machinations of ordinary life, it nonetheless proceeds by its own odd logic, largely conducted by the witchy Madelaine, though her motives remain squirrely. She desires Elaine, Elaine supposes, and wishes to both possess and destroy her, to make her part of the game, rather than its main target. Kraf's fascination with disordered and fragmentary mental states might signal that Madelaine has only ever been a conjured antagonist that Elaine requires to battle her own psychic splitting. Eventually, though, the two are fused: Mad/Elaine becomes one.

—

Politically and creatively, the late sixties and seventies were an electrifying era for women artists. Fairy tales and children's fables animated some of the decade's most ideologically and formally radical—not to mention radically *erotic*—feminist literature. Title IX was passed in '72; Roe v. Wade was decided in '73. As consciousness-raising groups facilitated coalition building through personal testimony, many women sought to dismantle culturally inescapable myths. What had these Ur-texts of their youth trained them to believe about 'proper' femininity, domestic labor, sexual pleasure, marriage, and motherhood? Who counts, in such stories, as a *good* girl or a *good* woman?

In the United States and Canada, Anne Sexton's 1971 poetry collection, *Transformations*, and Margaret Atwood's 1969 novel, *The Edible Woman*, redrew the horizons of female experience in "adult" revisions of stories made mythic by the Brothers Grimm. Toni Morrison interpolated Zerna Sharp and William S. Gray's "Dick and Jane" reading series into *The Bluest Eye* (1970) to interrogate the indoctrination of children into racist and sexually exploitative belief systems. Maxine Hong Kingston's *The Woman*

Warrior—which blended autobiography with Chinese folktales—
was published in '76. *The House of Madelaine* is, in some vital
sense, a phantasmic screed against the trappings of heterosexual
marriage.

On the desire women feel for men outside of marital bounds,
Kraf is ambivalent. We'd do well to remember it's Florence's love
of Gerard that gets the women into this mess in the first place.
Moreover, Elaine's infatuation with Joseph acts as a kind of in-
tellectual anesthetic: Once she starts fucking him, she loses sight
of her alliance with Florence and of the world outside the house's
gray, lockless door. When Elaine begins selling sex in the basement, her "trouble"—if trouble it must be called—is an inability
to divorce the act from emotion. Her sexual sincerity is anti-
thetical to the desires of her clients: "It was to annihilate the self
through pure erotic experience that they came to me." Joseph
gives her a manual; he attempts to instruct her in "the science of
non-involvement." Despite her grief over having lost his affec-
tions, she must learn not to look to sex for love any longer. She
must learn to depersonalize, or else be punished.

It's easy to extract an anti-sex work interpretation of Elaine's
time in the makeshift brothel, but Kraf's sense of her heroine's
participation is more complicated. If Elaine recoils from the impersonality of the encounters and her own meticulously crafted
sensual alienation, the brothel is also the place where Elaine
masters the sexual personae that enable her to liberate herself
from Joseph's debasements. In so doing, she further overcomes
Madelaine's iron grip around her throat, in turn supplanting the
other woman as the head of the house. Though this transformation does not manifest any wondrous feminist utopias, Elaine's
experience in sex work is nevertheless inextricable from a
broader project of self-making. Transactional sex and cultural
mythologies of "prostitution" are only more master narratives;
Elaine can just as easily discard or revolutionize the erotic manual Joseph imposes on her. And in reckoning with systems of

female sexual subservience—while committing to a revisionary procedure of participating in these erotic performances—Elaine's buried memories of wifely trauma surface.

Marriage, for Kraf, appears as an ineradicably patriarchal institution engineered to discipline women in our capacities as erotically, intellectually, and gynecologically autonomous beings. In our 21st-century moment of so-called heteropessimism—and within the present literary ecosystem's fascination with divorce narratives—*The House of Madelaine* feels shockingly current despite being, in part, a historical document of the sexual and institutional upheavals of the late 20th century. Though being pimped out by her lover leaves Elaine stricken, sex work enables her, in some slantwise fashion, to unearth her past and so (one hopes) eventually undo its damage.

For there is a husband haunting her history, after all: "I wanted to say, 'husband'; there was no word. I held up the gold ring and threw it on the floor." Elaine has fled the man—or possibly murdered him. During her trial for the manslaughter of Alfred, she confesses that "I've killed no one, except a gynecologist . . . and surely that's not a crime." Recollections of her marriage to the shadowy doctor surface in fragments: Elaine is inspected, prodded, repositioned, and altered. She is reduced to a vessel or instrument for his desire, his genitals, his experimentations. "He abducted my legs," Elaine admits.

It still shocks me to be reminded that spousal rape wasn't outlawed in the United States until '74; loopholes still exist in some states today. For Elaine, stealing Madelaine's crown to play the dictator does not free her from the house; it only reproduces the same interpersonal inequities and existential tedium. Facing her demons is all that remains. "I know that they, my silencers, are only my phantoms." Spectral or not, the wounds throb. After Roe, post-#MeToo, and in an alarmingly misogynistic political age, such "historical" horrors no longer peer back at us from the periphery of sexual life; again, abjection and subordination are its center. Fairy tales persist because they unearth or grant shape to commonplace and even discursively universalized human experiences. This does not mean they are immutable, or that the outcomes imagined in them are fated. As Kraf knew, we mustn't lose sight of transformation. We must rewrite our worst stories. We must go on dreaming other worlds.

———

JAMIE HOOD is the author of the memoir *Trauma Plot*. She is also the author of *How to Be a Good Girl*, one of *Vogue*'s Best Books of 2020, and *regards, marcel*, a monthly newsletter on Proust and other miscellany. Her essays and criticism have appeared in *The Baffler*, *Bookforum*, *The Nation*, the *Los Angeles Review of Books*, *The New Inquiry*, *The Drift*, and elsewhere. She lives in Brooklyn.

PART ONE

Once beyond the gate, we passed through a long aisle of dark bushes. They crossed, hiding the top of a house whose existence was confirmed by a wooden door, freshly painted gray. The door handle was black. And the door was not locked. (There was, in fact, no place for a key.) It waited only the faint pressure of her slim fingers. Florence's white-gloved hand was silent around the handle. She looked at me, but I stared straight ahead.

"I hope Gerard doesn't forget to meet me here," she said.

I didn't tell her that I had already glimpsed Gerard and Madelaine behind huge fir trees, taking notes and planning minute movements.

"If he forgets . . . ," she whimpered, pulling a white half-veil over her blinking eyes.

Then she stood up very straight as she did when trying to gain control of a volatile class. Without looking at me she pressed the lever underneath the handle and quickly pushed open the door.

The vestibule was a long corridor painted a vile shade of pale green. Several formica-topped tables rested against the walls on either side. Except for two, they were unoccupied. Neither occupant seemed to notice our entrance despite the sound of our high heels on the limestone floor.

"This is my mother," Florence indicated, stopping in front of a motionless figure bent over a table top.

"Mother, I'd like you to meet Elaine." At the end of this effort her voice faltered and she wiped her eyes with a tiny lace handkerchief that she pulled from her purse.

"She never answers me," sobbed Florence. Then, forgetting my presence, she disappeared behind one of the doors at the corridor's terminal. I assumed that she went to search for Gerard. I hoped that, free of Madelaine, he was waiting for her.

Florence's mother remained motionless except for the incessant movement of her third finger and thumb as they twisted a few strands of greasy gray-brown hair. (These bony fingers never ceased during my entire stay in the house.) Nor did they stop as she suddenly looked up. Furry eyes protruded from heavy, discolored sockets.

"Elaine, would you mind changing the water."

She referred to a small, pleated paper cup which held two inches of water and four pansies, all yellow with brown centers. She deftly removed each pansy from the cup and laid it carefully on the table. I picked up the drinking cup. The water was perfectly fresh. She directed me to a water fountain, not more than a few feet away. I pressed the pedal and filled the cup two and one quarter inches full. Then I replaced it in front of her. Without a word she submerged the pansies, and resumed staring into them.

Her lack of grace irritated me. "Why don't you answer when Florence speaks to you?" I accused in a tone of indignation. A slight smile passed over her jaundiced face.

At the end of the narrow corridor was the wider terminus, with three doors, freshly painted gray. The door behind which Florence had disappeared was the one on the left. It opened for a moment, and she stared down the length of the corridor to where her mother sat. She still held the crumpled handkerchief in her hand. Her face was pale, and the movements of her eyelids were more rapid than before.

As I walked toward her the door closed. "Gerard, Gerard," I heard from behind the door until it grew too faint to understand.

I wanted to reach beyond this door, to take her hand and lead her away from this house. It offered only disintegration to the self she had painstakingly created. Who would answer her? What would become of the plaintive call; of Florence, a tenuous composition of veils, lace, and white gloves.

I wanted to lead her to safety but I was unable to free myself from the will of Madelaine, who I knew was hidden behind some false door or window. She had already prepared a series of traps to make my exit unlikely. Of this I was certain.

I continued slowly down the corridor examining the pansies that filled countless white drinking cups. I looked to the left and right, under tables and behind chairs. I tapped the walls for secret doors leading to sub-corridors in which Madelaine and other members of her society might be waiting.

Underneath the sixth formica-topped table there crouched a skinny man in a custom-tailored black dress suit with a tight satin vest, also black. His nails were carefully shaped, and covered with iridescent lacquer. He was bent over rows of blue-lined filing cards, arranging them in a particular order.

"The empty cards are most important," he said without looking at me. (I had seated myself on the floor next to him, frozen with curiosity.) "But of course you knew that immediately, being such an intelligent young lady."

"Aren't you Mr. Blatt, the principal of P.S. X?" I asked timidly.

"Why no, and who might you be . . . but of course this is such a large family that I may have forgotten. There are always new ones coming in. Perhaps it is you who has stolen . . . oh never mind. You see, if you correctly calculate, there are ways to admonish all of them without too much risk, or damage if you prefer. But you would naturally understand or misunderstand the rules of discipline, being a disciple of . . . what was his name again?"

"I am Florence's friend. My name is Elaine. I taught kindergarten at P.S. X."

"Kindly concentrate, if you please. Teachers tend to write too much in the wrong order. And the worst teachers use green ink. I assure you. In my school no one is permitted to write with green ink."

"Aren't you the principal of P.S. X?"

"It's all a bluff and the business of precise minds to put in order what has been dismembered. You see, it's a proverb—my own, one of my own—that those who have most to say write least. So I am putting them first in line. I don't adhere to the notion of size places. But a little competition never hurt anyone. If you behave yourself I'll give you a pedicure and a permanent. Mrs. Fraudleman, who writes nothing, and has in fact not filled in any information is first. A less astute mind might put her last."

He indicated rows of blue-lined cards that extended all the way down to the side door through which Florence had vanished.

"These cards are duplicates and triplicates. It saves time later. The more efficient a teacher, the more duplicates and triplicates I have for her. Efficiency has to do with lack of expressiveness. I loathe expression. Not that I make value judgments. Heavens, no. If you behave yourself I'll give you a pedicure. But when all is said and done, as so it must, things work out in sequences."

Abruptly he pulled a pink envelope out of his inside vest pocket. My name was clearly printed across it in a floral hand I recognized as Gerard's.

"A gentleman named Gerard left a message I am to give to someone if she proves her identity beyond a reasonable doubt."

"I am Elaine. Did he pass this way?"

"I can give out no information until I have positive proof of your identity."

"Who else could I be?" I asked with exasperation. He stopped working for a moment to consider this.

"You might be a teacher and in that case have no right to assume identities. It is an affront and an impertinence to be a teacher and claim legal right to information."

He put the pink envelope back inside his vest pocket. Then he shuffled several cards.

"Some teachers fill out their cards in French. I think that worthy of separate consideration. Either they must be rewarded or fired." He began to assemble the cards that were written in French.

I approached Florence's mother, who was regarding the pansies with concentration.

"Please tell my principal that I am Elaine."

"Elaine, would you mind changing the water."

After I had changed the water and she had replaced the pansies, I returned to demand of Mr. Blatt the information left by Gerard. But he was no longer underneath that or any other table. Except for one card, there was no trace of his labor. It was printed in green ink, filled from top to bottom and bore the name ELAINE. I began to cry, seated before the isolated card that I had printed so carefully and informatively in elegant green ink.

For the first time, I began to consider the possibility of escape. It would mean breaking a promise. Florence had begged me to escort her to her family's house, and I had promised not to leave until she was united with Gerard.

But where was Gerard hidden? How long could I witness her gradual dissolution as she searched, in vain, behind gray doors? And how many times would her mother make me freshen the water in the pleated cup?

This unending task and my confinement in the green corridor had become onerous. At any moment my principal might return and question my efforts at discipline and self-control. He and the powerful Madelaine could make a brutal attack, in duplicate, upon my psyche—here where disorientation made me defenseless. Fearing her heavy footsteps and the swishing of her black taffeta slips, I began walking toward the gray door which I believed to be unlocked. Another day I would return and rescue Florence.

I had passed the mother, whose attention was fixed inside the sticky pistil of a pansy, and was approximately four feet from the door. From a side corridor I hadn't noticed before, there appeared a man whose attractiveness caused me to stop. I lost all thought of reaching the door. Madelaine's society had done their research well. Not all the real or imagined terrors of the green corridor would have made me leave it.

"I am Florence's brother," he said. I was astonished. During the two years that Florence and I had been friends she had never mentioned a brother.

"We are twins," he added, noticing how I scrutinized his features.

"As you can see," said a deep rasping voice from the direction of the last pansy cup I had freshened, "they are not identical. Joseph made his entrance last; almost two minutes after she appeared. Joseph dear, see to dinner." He kissed her forehead and she withdrew once more.

I was trembling, transfixed.

So often had I described, pointed out to Florence the exact image of the lover I desired. As we traveled from one convention to another, seated in the lobby of a hotel or on the barstool of a crowded cocktail lounge, I selected the trim of the beard from one, the strong, finely shaped hands from another, and the eyes which probed with an intensity somewhere between brilliance and madness from a third. Part by part, in this way, I had constructed the visual image that coincided with Joseph.

Had she maliciously withheld him from me? Or was some monstrous joke being played, at my expense, by Madelaine? Was it possible that Florence, weakened by love, had betrayed me and given Gerard the necessary information?

But his presence had already surrounded me. I could not keep my negative conjectures in focus.

"Come into my studio and rest before dinner," he said, guiding me gently to the right door at the end of the corridor. As I walked I felt my toes hitting something softer than limestone. Glancing at the floor I saw wilting pansies strewn everywhere. I tried, but I could not avoid stepping on them.

I fell in love instantly with Joseph's room. A high bed was topped with an apricot-colored canopy fringed with white. The bedspread matched. Soft yellow rugs of many tones from butter to hazelnut covered the parquet. Under the bed lived a brown cat. When he secluded himself from his family, under lock and key, she kept him company. He kept the key to this room on a silver ring attached to his belt.

There were no windows in Joseph's room, but two false windows, covered with maroon drapes held dying cactus plants on the fake sills. The walls were covered with book shelves extending from ceiling to floor. They housed every art book I had dreamed of possessing. (I could retreat into the artificial depths or harsh frontal planes of paintings.)

Joseph lit amber lamps.

I looked at his desk. In addition to a multitude of dissertation notes, articles for publication, and a diary of current dreams, there were index cards, steel-gray file boxes, and abandoned typewriter ribbons. I shuddered—the result of fear and pleasure because of my fatal attraction to art historians.

"I am an art historian," he said while handing me a small glass of apricot brandy. I sipped it, no longer conscious of Madelaine or Gerard, nor aware of the green corridor lined with formica-topped tables.

After making sure that I was comfortable, he left through an opening in the center of the floor. It was ordinarily covered by a beige rug. The cat followed.

At the foot of the stairway which wound for quite a distance, I could see a huge kitchen. Thirty men wearing purple hats and aprons were busy at work. I watched them stirring huge pots of soup and taking frozen flanks of meat from gigantic refrigerators. Blue flames shot up, and I heard the sizzling sound of boiling broth.

Reassured by these sights and sounds, I replaced the rug over the trap door and sat back against the bedstead, anticipating all the pleasures to come. The amber light, art history books, and brandy soothed me. Nor did an occasional rasping laugh or the sound of shuffling cards disturb my quiet.

An hour passed and Joseph had not returned. To entertain myself, I began opening and closing books, turning pages and studying inscriptions. I wanted to search the drawers. But they were locked. The clothing closet was open. I expected to see Joseph's coats; to examine a variety of ties and select my favorites. Or to search inside pockets for small notations and snapshots.

Instead I found dozens of freshly laundered costumes. All were carefully pressed and glistened with fake jewels. There was a yellow polka-dotted clown's suit, Elizabethan gowns with boned corsets, Revolutionary wigs, naval officers' uniforms, leotards, feathered ballet skirts, and draped togas from ancient Rome. Each garment was marked with a tag. Small, Medium, or Large was carefully printed in green ink. I tried on the exquisitely jeweled gowns, but they were tailored for gigantic women. Two choices remained: an ordinary nurse's uniform and an underwater diving suit. Both were labeled Small. I switched from one to the other in great haste; black fins to white oxfords and back to black fins. I was afraid Joseph would return before I had finished dressing. Finally I chose the nurse's uniform. I hung up my turquoise shift in its place and closed the closet door. As I was doing this, a wheezing sound caught my attention.

"Help me, nurse." It was Gerard's voice from below.

I found the square in the floor that slid open and climbed

down to what had been a kitchen. It was indeed Gerard, disguised as a cook, who lay wheezing on a cot. His cook's hat was on the floor. Perspiration came out of his pores.

"Nurse, I need adrenalin," he said, taking my hand. But Gerard couldn't deceive me that easily. I knew that he was a leading figure in the conspiracy against me. I also was acquainted with his gift for drama. Prior to his literary career, he had played dozens of leading roles in Broadway productions. I watched indifferently as he wheezed and gasped for breath.

"What have you done with Florence?" I accused in a self-righteous voice. (The presence of her twin had eclipsed her from my consciousness. Since the initial annoyance I had experienced at her withholding of Joseph, I hadn't given her a thought.)

"She wouldn't have come here if it wasn't for your influence," I continued. "It was only to find you that she passed through the corridor."

"It was you who made her entrance possible," he gasped. "How else would she have gotten the courage to open the gray door?"

Gerard was right. I had warned and cautioned her. But only to appease my conscience. I knew that Florence feared her mother beyond all things. But Madelaine had reached me despite my protestations. (Gerard understood my hypocrisy.) With the excuse of supporting and protecting Florence, I had agreed to enter the house. Gerard knew that I, only I could have dissuaded her. But in spite of the risk, particularly to Florence, I could not help myself from entering the house of her family.

As I moved toward Gerard, the wheezing became more distinct. I heard the sound of conjested phlegm and put my ear to his chest. The thick sound was really coming from within. I remembered that Gerard was asthmatic. He had many such attacks in Madelaine's literary class. I reached into the pocket of my uniform and withdrew a hypodermic syringe which I boiled in a pot of water on one of the few large stoves still surrounding us.

"Where is the adrenalin kept?" I asked Gerard. He made a sign to indicate that there was none.

"Call the doctor quickly." He was hardly breathing, and turning blue.

"Doctor," I called and waited. I called again and heard footsteps.

Joseph appeared, looking pale. His white coat was stained with blood—from the dinner he was preparing, I assumed. Or else he was already carving the roast. Without a glance at me, he approached Gerard and felt his pulse.

"Nurse, is the hypodermic syringe sterilized?" he asked.

"Yes, doctor," I answered, handing it to him. "I thought you were an art historian."

"Quiet," he ordered.

I stepped back. And as I did so the walls seemed to recede. Joseph and Gerard became minute.

"Everything is moving away," I shouted. But it was too late. They were so far away they looked like toys I could hold in my hand. I could no longer hear the wheezing. I assumed that the adrenalin was moving through Gerard's veins.

———

I awoke in Joseph's amber-lit study. The relationship of one size to another had adjusted itself. I checked sizes; the door in relation to the clock, my hand relative to the door, the cat compared to me. There was no window in Joseph's room, so I could not check the relationship between the window and the door.

Joseph's back was toward me. He was bent over a book of medieval paintings. From my bed I could see a black-robed figure, her finger to her eye. She sat against a background of gold. Four angels hovered above, holding a crown over her head.

"Where is my uniform? I mean my dress; the turquoise shift flecked with crescents?"

He did not answer. Instead he turned and smiled at me. As he came nearer to my bed I stared at the pale, onyx-ringed fingers which I hoped would soon touch me. He sat on the edge of the bed and took my hand between both of his.

"This will be our bed from now on," he whispered. Then he went to the closet and brought out a blue kimono with small yellow roses.

"Wear this to dinner. It will be very beautiful on you." He dressed me in the blue fabric and held me close to him.

"Don't be afraid. Be whatever you feel at the moment. There is no need for pretense," he said, leading me from the room.

We entered the banquet hall. The table was elegantly set for nine. It was covered with a beige cloth. The centerpiece was a white bowl filled with yellow pansies.

—

Gerard, fully recovered but wearing the cook's uniform, was seated to my left. Next to him was Florence, naked except for the veil which still covered her eyes. She held the lace-trimmed handkerchief in her hand and smiled happily, holding Gerard's hand underneath the table. Hannah, the lady poet, who wore the symbol of copulation around her waist, was seated next to Mr. Blatt.

"Elaine, this is my uncle, Alfred Blatt," said Joseph, indicating the principal.

"How do you do." Alfred extended his hand, fingers stained with green ink. I tried to catch Florence's eye across Gerard, to see if she recognized our former principal. But she sat with a fixed smile, her eyes not seeing me.

"Florence, have you called Mother?" Joseph asked.

"You know that your mother doesn't answer her," I said, astonished by his thoughtlessness.

Just then a rasping voice was heard outside the door.

"Come along, Madelaine."

"Is it time already? Have you wound the clock?"

The voice was familiar. I shuddered as the door opened, revealing the green corridor, as Madelaine, dressed in black, and Florence's mother entered.

"She's wearing my dress," I said, seeing my turquoise shift hanging on the bony figure, its gray crescents glittering in the lamplight.

But Joseph motioned me to be silent. He seemed to have control of the situation.

"I've had this dress for seventeen years," rasped Florence's mother. "It's my favorite dress."

Madelaine sat between Florence's mother and Hannah. She did not greet me. And in that respect things were exactly as they had been in the literary class. Hannah, touching the symbol of copulation, looked at me and smiled conspiratorily at Gerard. A warning glance from Madelaine made her stop.

"That's a pretty kimono, Elaine," remarked Hannah.

"Yes," echoed several voices.

Everyone had begun to eat when Madelaine observed that there was an unoccupied seat. Each stopped eating his grapefruit and waited.

"Go ahead," urged Joseph, but since he did not lift his spoon we refrained.

"The more grapefruits eaten, the less teachers there are bound to be. Therefore I will eat mine," said Alfred.

Then he ate the grapefruit in front of the unoccupied seat. "That's two teachers done away with."

"He ate Father's grapefruit," whimpered Florence, reaching underneath her veil with the lace handkerchief. Gerard, who really loved her, patted her hand and whispered something comforting into her ear. I felt happy for her and prayed that her wedding day was not far in the distant future.

As the clock struck nine, magisterial music was heard. Joseph's father entered, wearing a purple cape lined with gold dust. His beard hung heavy and white. On his feet were ordinary house slippers. The socks he wore were striped, brown and white. Almost hiding them were the tattered bottoms of cuffless gray tweed trousers.

"At last the magician is here," said the woman wearing my dress. Or I said it.

Florence's hand slipped out of the cook's as she ran to embrace her father, Sir Phalatrope. He smiled kindly at all of us and gave a benediction. That made everyone feel more hospitable. Madelaine smiled at me, exposing artificial teeth. "Don't take it all so seriously," was the meaning I derived from this contact. Was I included in the game after all, rather than being its main target? I felt hopeful as we devoured our meal.

———

After dinner we filed into the corridor. Alfred fell asleep under his favorite table, his cards scattered about. Gerard and Florence chatted in a corner, oblivious of anyone else. Joseph, the host, offered coffee, or apricot brandy if we preferred.

Hannah decided to read her own poem aloud. I listened politely.

> There comes a time
> In the hearts of men
> When the clocks are
> Wound too tight
> Then they must give in
> Lest the heart divide
> Let the gander fly
> In the Western sky.

> There comes a time
> In the lives of men
> When the clocks are wound
> And they count to ten
> Then away they fly

Lest the heart divide
And the mushroom die
In the darkened sky.

For the heart has wings
As well as springs
And well it knows
The dark divide
Where the river ends
And the darkness lies.

There comes a time
When all time is a lie
And to trust the clock
Is to crush the wing
For all love lies
In the dark divide
Where the river ends
And the senses fly.

Then she twirled the insignia of copulation and smiled as Sir Phalatrope and Madelaine looked up from their conversation to applaud. After the applause there was stillness. The mother, wearing my turquoise dress, stared into the pansies. The sight of my dress caused a feeling of panic inside me. I glanced at the gray door at the beginning of the corridor. But Joseph was instantly at my side, reminding me of the delights he had for me behind the door of my amber room. He bent over to kiss me as I sat staring into the sticky pistil of a pansy. His moustache smelled like fresh grass.

—

As the weeks passed, all desire to approach the gray door disappeared. Each evening I went to sleep in Joseph's arms, and when I awoke I smelled the hair on his chest. Knowing that in some other room Florence lay similarly in Gerard's arms, my guilt was lessened. (I still felt to blame for the suffering she endured trying to contact her mother.) At least once a day I saw her standing over the motionless woman, talking and wiping the tears which streamed from beneath her veil.

I realized that Madelaine had a magician to assist her. And that I was in her power. But she had not known, I assumed, that Florence's brother would be by my side, in my bed, a buffer between myself and her evil imagination.

If I was scribbling sentences in a quiet corner, a shadow would fall upon the page. Without warning, she hovered above the floor, floating through space, black-sheathed arms waving like wings.

"Your words are refuse—a collage of floral embroidery. There is no character analysis or plot," she would state in her husky voice. Then she would remain suspended there until I threw the page to the floor. With a husky laugh she departed.

At odd moments she assaulted me, her dark wrath following me from room to room until it exploded in a rainbow of unending suggestion.

"Even he is in the plot against you," she whispered, suspended near the ceiling. Joseph slept peacefully, unaware of her presence. But I remained awake, trying to keep the distance between us. If I slept she might swoop down and smother me with her electric taffeta, or come between Joseph and Elaine, who were asleep in each other's arms.

"I am the soul's death, the power that turns clocks, causes the stars to form certain constellations—the sun drowns in my bosom," she would whisper to me when no one was listening. And I would tremble, feeling the rich infection invading my blood.

The purple-robed magician became blurred and impotent when Madelaine attacked me. In vain did I search for him in the haze that her presence created.

"The magician is stronger," I whispered to myself although I did not really believe it, since he remained remote and when he spoke his words were in a language I couldn't translate.

"Dear Sir Phalatrope, why do you speak to me in that distant tongue? Madelaine speaks loudly and clearly. She bends close to my ear and each word makes a permanent indentation in my brain."

He answered in a language of his own. It was full of b's, l's, and g's, and sounded like "blugged, glibbed blugen, blog."

THE MAGICIAN VISITS ME

Everyone had coupled off, comfortably. Florence and Gerard were seldom seen in public. Except for sudden glimpses of Florence, in doorways, trying to contact her mother, and secret messages left by Gerard (which I could seldom get possession of), I lost contact with them. They stopped coming to our dinners. Joseph explained that under the circumstances it was best that way, thus I needn't concern myself. I always believed Joseph. So I no longer worried about Florence.

Uncle Alfred, who I would no longer swear was Principal Blatt of P.S. X, and Hannah were constant companions. They were in the same room simultaneously, she reciting poetry, he inventing proverbs. Although there was not much direct communication, it was evident that there was a growing empathy between them. Their mutual joy was heightened by sharing rooms together. Hannah wrote her finest poetry during this period of her life. At our dinners she always offered her best poem of the day. We applauded heartily. Even Madelaine smiled or cried, as the poem demanded.

However, I observed in Madelaine a subtle but mounting anger at this pairing off. It was insulating important candidates against her attacks. We were less available for her conferences. She had to distribute her maps through secret channels, assuming that they arrived.

Her constant companion was Florence's father, Sir Phalatrope.

I knew that to a great extent my fate as well as Florence's was in the hands of the magician. Therefore the influence he exerted over Madelaine was very important. But as far as I could discern, he liked her exactly as she was.

At bizarre, incredible hours, I heard them giggling, sharing jokes behind walled partitions. Or else they sat together in the endless green hall, playing chess or doing crossword puzzles. Occasionally I caught them shaking a paperweight and staring into it as white fluttered down the curves of the crystalline. Sometimes long white hairs adhered to the sleeves of her black satin dress. Or gold dust fell down between the crack of her enormous bosom.

Joseph left our room quite often, either through the floor panel to attend to preparations in the kitchen below, or through a doorway that led to the corridor. At first I thought that a vestibule separated me from that part of the house. But I discovered that the back of the headboard was adjacent to the back of the chair on which his mother sat. It was this exit he used to make his frequent visits to her. He visited her many times a day, more often than I liked. (I found squashed pansies stuck to the soles of his shoes. Or he blatantly placed one in the closed button of his shirt.) Sharing Joseph was one of the things I found hardest to become resigned to.

However, it was on one of Joseph's urgent visits with his mother that I felt the full impact of the great Sir Phalatrope.

I was amusing myself, as usual, by trying on various costumes that appeared and disappeared from my closet. With regularity old ones were replaced by those that were brand new, or those I had worn a long time ago. I never understood the poverty of my choice. It puzzled me that among the hundred costumes, only two were labeled Small. (One of two choices is most difficult to make.)

On the day of Sir Phalatrope's appearance, my choice was narrowed down to a feathery dress with a duck's bill or a traditional witch's gown.

The witch's costume fit perfectly. It was made of satin-taffeta, not unlike the shimmering cloth of Madelaine's dress. The hat was two feet high. I felt bold and hideous in this outfit and was laughing gleefully when a door opened in the back of the closet and the magician crawled from beneath costumes. He was wearing his purple cape and an old pair of faded green trousers. Underneath his arm was a package tied with red ribbon.

"I have brought blue a bleegen," he said, seating himself on the floor. He was smiling as I tore it open. It was a large photograph of a house that I did not recognize.

"Thank you," I said politely. "Should I remove my hat?"

"Og, og. Ig beleg been bly of witches. When I heard that a gugblye witch was leeging here, I bloughten keep away. Do blue bun the lone lion in bloom of the nin? I larved it long an ordinary front snail. As blue can bun, it has a boman's leagts; a Chimaera, blue bligen dig. It bug a bleegen for my life on our ligth anniversary."

"I don't know this house."

"The blunen blue don't blegorine the nin is that the nilges have blewg so long that only the boog is visible. The fliggens are blef green and pansies blew in window lipens beneath. Eg is also a gon blye white horse in bloom of the boog. I larved it igle. It's a hitching glot. Poolooged, in didn't fog out in this shot. Eng, it's the lost important thing."

"But this door is rectangular and the brass knocker has a cat's head. It couldn't be this house." I remembered the curved top of the gray door and the ordinary handle that Florence's gloved hand had rested upon long ago.

My disbelief made him laugh. "Particularly to flitches and glitches, pones are not what they glibe. It gliggens them, of all peenin. But to magicians it's gugblye that leg. I don't blyt to fleeb what will blogen or flupe will be in any piggen ninet." He laughed and seemed to want me to join in.

Obligingly I laughed.

"Og, og," he roared. "Flitches aren't supposed to be so dooglen. Blue are very biglouggeting." He stared at me thoughtfully while stroking his beard. "Slot, I'm blyneeged du gleeven blue fluggen. Remember to glit this photolag shugged—what is in in, as lig as what is bleeged but. Eng, don't be afloog to be a flitch or glogen a duck if blue blyt. Blue bun," he said, shaking his head sadly, "she's no glabben life for a magician, pelleg ligged, never changing, gonnun moving. ul slot . . ." He kissed my forehead and disappeared into the closet leaving gold dust sparkling on the rug. I lay on it and fell asleep.

I dreamed that Madelaine sat on a huge throne covered with gray and silver crescents. Sir Phalatrope knelt before her. Then he crowned her with a diadem such as the angels held over Mary in Joseph's book of medieval painting. Ecstatic laughter came from both of them. He slid into her, lifting the turquoise silk above her knees. And the knees of Madelaine were young and smooth.

"Stop laughing." It was Joseph bending over me, his white jacket stained with blood, either from the meat he was cooking or an operation he was performing. He held a surgical instrument. It looked familiar . . . but I couldn't place it.

"Please don't shout at me, Joseph," I begged. He removed my witch's hat and gave me a hypodermic of Sodium Pentothal. It made me relax.

"We are having a special event after tonight's dinner," I heard him say. The last thing I saw before the injection took full effect was the photograph of the house. I stared at its black, rectangular door. I thought of the invisible white horse upon whose back I would soon be carried away.

———

"Pass the marmalade," demanded Alfred.

"There is no marmalade," Hannah whispered, her long fingers nervously twisting the symbol of copulation she had removed from her waist.

"Which of you is responsible?" Alfred asked, eyeing each of us with suspicion. "I know that teachers steal rubber bands and board erasers for spite. I keep careful count of paper clips and rubber bands. Last year 99,362 rubber bands were stolen by eight teachers. Then one of them went too far. She took needles, thimbles, brown towels, and toilet paper. She must be the one who took the marmalade. I think it was the duck."

"There is no duck," I protested in vain.

"I will deprive that teacher of all water. Torture her for vandalism."

"I'll get you some marmalade, Uncle Alfred," Joseph soothed. Alfred gave a little bit to Hannah.

"Deprive the duck. Fire the teachers. Murder the thieves. My cards will show where you belong."

"Me?"

"Elaine, try not to personalize." Joseph did not mean to sound condescending. I am sure of that. Perhaps it was the position he was in that caused such tones to escape.

"Have you a poem for us this evening, Hannah?" he asked in the same tone.

She had the poem in her lap as usual. To everyone's annoyance, she decided to stand on her chair for the recitation.

"The effect of Alfred's marmalade, no doubt," snickered Madelaine to Sir Phalatrope.

"It was very generous of Alfred to share his marmalade with Hannah," interposed Joseph. "It proves that he is moving along."

"I dedicate this poem," said Hannah blushing.

> Wings of death
> Bells of cocks
> Cows shackles
> Hurt so much
> Blue lagoon
> Where I drown

Zippers slip
Wings of death.

Wings of snow
Bells of time
Blue lagoon
Zippers down
Hurts so much
Where I sit.

Bells of clocks
Blue lagoon
Where I drown
Hurts so much
Shackles freeze
Zippers down
Where I am
Time is dead.

We all clapped. Then Joseph announced the surprise.

"Instead of retiring to our rooms we are going to have a cel-ebration. It has been arranged by Madelaine and Sir Phalatrope."

I was not in the mood for a celebration. I whispered to Joseph that I would wait in our room. He felt, however, that my pres-ence at the event was indispensable, and my retreat out of the question. I was about to ask if Florence could come, but Made-laine was already taking control.

She led us through the corridor, her wings shining and whirl-ing, past pansies wilting in empty cups, to the room that she shared with Sir Phalatrope.

It was a small black box with gold cushions on the floor. In the corner, also painted black, was an examining table with stirrups for high heels. From the ceiling hung objects whose functions I could not imagine, although I remembered their names. There were ropes, gauges, rolls of gauze, a gigantic tenaculum, thumb forceps, endometrial curettes, and a gleaming speculum.

Nor could I guess the nature of the ceremony. I looked at Joseph for clues, but he was escorting his mother to a gold cushion. Her turquoise dress was faded and stained with iodine.

Sir Phalatrope remembered me and winked as he took his place on an elevated platform next to Madelaine.

Madelaine of my dreams, of the death that clung to me since I first recognized her power over my mind; she had stood above me at the rostrum of her literary class. Gerard and Hannah, secret emissaries of my priestess, swore that her lectures dealt with style and form. They lied. I heard her voice instructing, demanding that I become immersed in the study of bizarre fetishists, and in the language of rape, murder, pederasty, incest, infanticide, suicide "by appointment," and necrophilia.

"Participate with your mind and senses in crime and aberration which represent the highest human exaltation," she whispered to me with dangerous invisible sense organs. Saliva flowing down her chin, eyes veiled behind glassless frames, she sent phosphorescent signals into our flesh. The others had obeyed gladly. Only I had resisted.

But here she was again, holding us captive in her black box, re-arranging our thoughts and calling the magician to help her.

Phosphorous eating my flesh, I cried out:

"Let me go. I cannot stay here."

Her eyes met mine, silencing me as before.

My strength against her presence in this house had come from the security I felt in Joseph's affection. But Joseph, I had already discovered, had times of preoccupation and withdrawal from me because of my vulnerability. It was the very thing he loved.

"The purpose of this game is to condition us to change." She smiled at the magician, who nodded approvingly and mumbled something in his own language. Then she lectured on the dangers of self-insulation and of partnerships which became incestuous from excluding all others. (I guessed her secret motives even then.) Her proposal was that we be re-paired for the evening, thus exchanging energies, breaking dependencies, and revitalizing ourselves. Joseph applauded this idea heartily while Hannah wept.

Alfred had agreed to devise a chance system of pairing based on the alphabet. Those with the most letters matching in their names would be partners. Sir Phalatrope and Joseph were paired. She, having my name enclosed in her own was to be my guide. Alfred and Florence were coupled, if he could find her. Hannah was told to search for Gerard. Joseph's mother remained alone.

Madelaine distributed her assignments in code. There was a variety of intricate maps with difficult routes to follow and enigmatic purposes to achieve.

The box turned over, expelling everyone but Madelaine and me. Joseph and Sir Phalatrope, leaving arm in arm, turned back and smiled encouragingly at me.

"They are my friends," I said, trembling and wheezing. She laughed and beckoned me to come closer.

"We will get down to brass tacks," she said, digging a finger into my arm. It left an acid stain.

"This is a wonderful place to live if you are willing to follow instructions. Everyone needs a plan and a logic so they do not disintegrate or fall prey to love. Therefore each crime must be committed in order."

She handed me a mimeographed list with a description of my assignments.

"You must believe," she advised me, "that these crimes will have no negative consequences for you; they are essential to your survival."

The three atrocities listed were: 1. Take Gerard from Florence. 2. Murder Alfred. 3. Destroy Joseph.

"When you have committed these acts you will be free."

"I will not murder and destroy," I said. The words suspended themselves in mid-air, hung on the blinding tenaculum, and fell to the dead-black floor.

Madelaine did not glower. Nor did she laugh derisively. She maintained, instead, concentration devoid of guile.

"Only through attack can you find out who you are. Love and pacifism are lies when born of self-ignorance."

I pleaded with Madelaine. I begged her to find an alternative solution. She smiled, gloating with self-confidence.

"The dimensions of this house have already shaped your response. Did you think you could hide forever from the violence inside you?"

Then she began to chuckle to herself. And I noticed the luster in her eyes. Saliva trickled down her chin.

She was unable to resist feasting on succulent images that formed in her brain as she observed the beginning symptoms of my submission.

"Everyone knows you want the magician for the ends I have prescribed," she said, floating above, resting upon the grotesque probing instruments that hung there bat-like, infusing her phosphorous with the metals.

"I will escape you," I said, looking way up into the formless black of her skirts. Deep within my blood I felt the hooves of the magic horse; he was waiting for me at the end of the aisle of trees outside the corridor.

—

I was propelled through a series of hallways that I feared would lead back to her. At times a gust of electricity lifted me off the floor and wafted me in its own fury. Other times I struggled, carrying iron weights on my head.

"Sir Phalatrope," I called.

"You must find the way yourself," he answered in my own tongue.

—

I reached my bedroom safely and found Joseph in bed. He was not sleeping. His eyes were fixed on the ceiling. When I entered he turned toward the wall. He had left the dimmest light burning for me, but he had turned away. It was as though he guessed the evil I carried inside. Not a word did he answer when I begged him to talk with me, nor did he move closer when I caressed him.

"What have I done?" I asked, sensing that his change was permanent.

When I finally fell asleep I dreamed that the white horse spat upon me, stamping my body with his hooves.

"I must contact the magician."

—

When I awoke Joseph was gone. His desk had been cleared. All amber lamps had vanished. I noticed blood stains on the butternut rug. They led to a corner beneath the canopied bed where lay the decapitated cat, still bleeding freshly from both parts.

There were no books to look at nor were there any costumes in the closet; I had nothing to do.

Feeling bored and very much alone, I opened the door behind the headboard. Of my own free will, I stepped into the vile green hall.

"Maid, come here and dust the tables," ordered Florence's mother who was usually silent. She twisted a strand of hair between her thumb and third finger while watching me with mocking eyes. How happy I was to have a title and a function. Tearing a piece of cloth from my kimono, I carefully wiped each table. Without being asked, I changed the water in each pansy cup. Too soon my tasks were completed.

"Have you seen Joseph today?" I asked, knowing that if she knew where he was she wouldn't tell me.

"Joseph has many functions here. I'm his mother." She laughed her rasping laugh. I noticed that her turquoise dress had faded so much that the crescents could no longer be seen.

I decided to search for Joseph. Then I would persuade him to return. He was the only person who could protect me from the acts dictated by Madelaine. With his help I could find a different way to leave the house.

Uncle Alfred was under the sixth formica-topped table, arranging cards. I approached him with caution, remembering the blueprint from Madelaine: MURDER ALFRED.

"Teachers who steal rubber bands must be punished, turned into ducks and roasted. No thief deserves a lover. Let me see, if six teachers times nine are late every morning and they are all under thirty, and if all teachers die at sixty that proves it. Something reprehensible is going on."

I swallowed my rage. "Joseph has disappeared. Do you know where he is?"

"Pass the marmalade, duck. And don't hide children in the museum. An intelligent teacher should be perfect. Fifty-four teachers are late every morning. Do you know what that means?" He stared into my eyes.

"I know what it means but I won't tell you," I said spitefully.

"Fine," he said. Then he handed me a pink envelope that he pulled from his inside vest pocket. TO ELAINE FROM GERARD was printed on it in a floral hand. I smiled at this testimony to my existence.

"Since you stole the marmalade I know you are Elaine. There is none worse."

I took the envelope, trembling with fury. MURDER ALFRED. I sat down at the eighth table and read it.

Dear Elaine,
I need your help in the kitchen tonight. Please don't disappoint me.

                                              Your
                                              Gerard.

I was glad to be acknowledged. Gerard's message cheered me. I hoped that he had news of Joseph. And our meeting was going to take place in the kitchen. This made me happy. The kitchen beneath the amber room always gave me a feeling of well-being. When Joseph slipped through the floorboard to descend, his absence did not disturb me. I pictured him directing the army of chefs, all moving in unison with lilac hats bouncing back and forth. When he returned stained with blood, I imagined the roast being carved by his deft fingers. Often on these evenings, when he was spattered with blood, there was no meat for dinner. But I had learned not to let these incongruities spoil this precious sense of the sublime. For what sublimity could not be found beneath the floorboard, down spiraling stairs, preparing mysteriously the moment of ecstasy.

Into the room which was no longer amber, but which held memories and expectancies still, I withdrew. I removed the floor panel and descended slowly into pitch blackness.

—

Had I made some mistake? Calling Joseph and then Gerard, I walked in darkness. I felt with my hand for the gigantic refrigerators where turkeys and ducks lay frozen. But even the stove, whose blue jets shot up wildly on other days, was not there. Had I come at the wrong time or on the wrong day and missed Gerard? Perhaps I had gone upstairs instead of down.

"Where is the white horse?" I called into black space.

"It will wait for you," answered a voice.

"Sir Phalatrope," I called, running blindly everywhere, my arms outstretched. No one stirred or tossed gold dust in my direction.

After what seemed like hours of wandering I decided to go back upstairs. The stairway that spiraled into my room was lost in darkness.

Exhausted, I fell asleep on a floor so cold it hurt my skin.

Sometimes a small mouse, also lost, scampered over my fingers or bumped against me by mistake and rushed away.

I dreamed that I sat on the huge lap of Sir Phalatrope. He wrapped me from head to toe in purple velvet robes. He tried to shelter me by wrapping the robes around me many times. At last I could not see or hear or breathe.

——

The sound of men and women's laughter awakened me. It was the forced gaiety of adults when they are having some festivity. I felt like a child awakened in the night; alone and alienated from these voices drifting over the other side of a wall. But their laughter was really separated from me only by a long expanse of space. Turning in the direction of the voices I saw the glow of a harsh red light. There was nothing to do but walk toward it. As I walked, afraid, I thought of Sir Phalatrope astride his horse waiting beyond the balsam firs. It would happen some day, after the dark layer broke apart. Amber lights had long replaced daylight. I did not know how long. But down here I thought nostalgically of piercing noon sunlight. Of the white light filtered through clouds revealing lovely textures on foggy afternoons. Whose fingers had I held on that dim afternoon watching the freight boats pass. There was something cold on my finger; metallic. It was no use. I could not remember any more.

In the darkness, made more bearable by distant light, Gerard came to meet me. He held out white-gloved hands while tears of tenderness and remorse fell down his cheek.

"I'm so sorry," he said. "I could have prevented the whole thing."

"No one could have prevented it," I answered, not knowing what I was saying.

"There can be no turning back now," he said with regret. "I must take you forward. Although I know some of the things we will find, I don't know all."

He held me tightly against himself. I felt the blue evening suit covering his long thighs and padding his bony shoulders. Then I moved back and looked into his eyes which were trying to blink out of the mist.

"Is Florence dead? Madelaine wants me to take you . . ." But he covered my next words with his gloved hand.

"Even Madelaine does not know everything that is about to happen."

"Will Joseph ever forgive me?"

He looked at me with pity. "You don't know Joseph."

"I do know. I know that Joseph is a doctor. We all know that, even though he pretends."

"Isn't he one of us?" said Gerard. Then he took my hand and led me over the cold floor, closer and closer to the noise and light. I held my hands over my ears, but Gerard removed them. Then he left me under the blaze of red light.

I saw about ten girls gyrating and writhing under the glare. They wore identical fuchsia costumes made of shiny satin. Tight bones pinched in their waistlines. And their breasts were pressed together, bulging over steel rims. They moved into red, and back toward shadow, attending to men with waxed moustaches and pin-striped suits. I thought they were mannequins, but I saw that the moustache roots grew from wet pores, and warm breath came from their nostrils and lips.

To these real wax men they served food, pausing to let a ruffled buttock bounce on a hard knee. Long muscular legs swathed in net kicked outward. As lacquered hands folded around corseted waists, the girls gracefully continued serving.

Joseph, in a tight blue suit with tiny yellow stripes running up his leg, patted the buttocks of a red-haired girl. As she joined a man poised over the pool table, he beckoned to me. I trembled as I crossed the floor, my faded robe turning red under harsh light, bumping into girls far prettier than I. Balanced on twelve-inch heels, they served drinks or sat thoughtfully at chessboards. I ran to Joseph, my hair disheveled and arms open.

"What have I done to make you move away?" I asked as he silently held me. I felt his icy fingers on my breasts and down my back. And he stared, not into my eyes, but at the long legs that crossed the floor brushing his trousers. With his right hand he cupped my breast. He ran his left hand around the boned waist of another girl, stopping her. The girl perched herself on his other knee, laughing softly as he fondled me. Then she stood before us swinging her hips and shaking her huge breasts until they fell out of the cups and hung over the red steel rims. Joseph jerked my breast faster, hurting it with his ice wax hand. Bored with this he ordered cocktails and watched the girl as she disappeared waving a feather that she held between her buttocks. The tears that fell from my eyes were strips of hot wax; I felt nothing. Nor did I see any need to protest his fingers. His eyes focused within; the dilated pupils reflected fragments of fuchsia silk like disengaged mirrors. He did not see me, but any minute it might change. The blue iris might appear once more, hiding those enlarged metallic discs. And he would look at me with warmth as he had when he first encountered me. I could not conceive of his affection being denied me forever, or that it could co-exist with this grotesque impersonality.

Sir Phalatrope appeared smoking a big cigar. His trousers were unwrinkled and an emerald glittered on his pinky. When he saw me he was sincerely shocked; I sat rocking rhythmically back and forth against Joseph's shoulder.

"How often must I explain the necessity of this rule—one must never mix business with pleasure. What is she doing here, Joseph?"

Joseph nodded in the direction of Gerard who was dancing with one of the girls.

"Let me glef blue du ble blye ninet," said Sir Phalatrope kindly.

"I want to stay here," I answered as Joseph shrugged and Sir Phalatrope wandered off, muttering to himself.

As the hours passed, I became accustomed to this wax replica of Joseph. I did not wonder how long he would remain at the formica-topped table with girls attending to him. I stared at the floor with eyes that did not blink. Sir Phalatrope leaned against the door watching us through a mirror. He wore a gray suit without a wrinkle. A tiny black tie came high on his throat, and a red carnation was inserted in his lapel. Beside him, on a walnut table, lay his flawless black derby with gray suede gloves resting on its rim. I noticed the fuchsia covered buttons on his vest. His shoes were so shiny that they reflected the girls' rumps as they passed. I wondered if he would call to me some day with a black saddle under his arms, his white beard combed; all ready for our journey.

Hypnotized by the shiny black leather, I went into a trance against Joseph's shoulder.

When my awareness returned, another girl was serving Joseph. I recognized the skinny legs hidden underneath net stockings. I looked up past the cinched-in waist and enormous hips to meet with my eyes the watery myopic eyes of my friend. She did not recognize me. She bent over Joseph, serving and being fondled exactly like the others.

Without a word she disappeared.

Later I saw her waiting and beckoning to me from a dark alcove behind her father. I left Joseph's table without his notice, and followed her. We went through the musty alcove into a small hot room lit by fluorescent tubes. Under these lights I examined my friend. I was alarmed by the dark shadows beneath her eyes and by her sickly pallor. An uncontrollable spasm twisted her facial muscles. Wrinkles and lines of fatigue appeared where the thick pancake solution cracked.

She did not speak. Instead, to my amazement, she held out to me a costume such as she wore.

"It is the only way. Believe me," she said, in a flat tone that I didn't recognize.

In the past I had been the more experienced, leading her to

acts born of a cynicism she would ordinarily have frowned upon. Now her voice and the twisting of her lips testified to resignations that I had not yet conceived of. However, I accepted the costume, gratefully discarding my kimono. We both stared at it for a second as it lay; a symbol of the dissolution of dreams.

In place of the robe, I dressed myself in the hideous contraption. It was made of materials so coarse that blotches appeared where it touched my skin. The stockings were of heavy mesh although they appeared flimsy from the distance. They stung my feet as I struggled to pull them up. I was having difficulty pulling the resistant material over my hips.

"Ease them up slowly," Florence directed. She witnessed my transformation with patient empathy.

Next came the bra over which my breasts hung, cut by the steel rim. Side clips pushed them together. (The room reeked from valiant efforts to create an illusion.) I felt faint from the confinement. But she encouraged me as an accomplice. Finally, I stepped into the built-up shoes and inserted the feather into my rectum, and out through a hole in the satin ruffles.

"With proper muscular control you can make the feather do as you please. Concentrate and never let go."

"But what has happened?" I asked, adding apologies and pieces of information about Madelaine's maps and missing amber lamps. I even nervously alluded to teaching, to blue ducks and purple-faced cooks.

"I know what you mean," she said absently. "But these changes are necessary." Her eyes blinked rapidly and a series of violent contractions distorted the left side of her face. Yet she smiled at me with encouragement. I knew that living with Gerard had brought her to this pathetic acceptance of fate. I never thought that Florence had so much strength. Encouraged by her forbearance, I allowed my costume to take over. I did not protest its restriction nor its vulgarity. Its anonymity disturbed me vaguely. But I needed this fuchsia tangibility.

Invaded by a strange exhilaration, I swung my hips gently, and entered the main room. I was as beautiful as anyone in my blonde wig. I smiled. Gerard met me, putting his arm around my riveted waist. He did not know that these rivets, gently flaring into graceful hips ate into my flesh making permanent striations. I held the feather with all my might as I walked. The sound of applause deafened me. There could be no doubt about it; I was the most beautiful girl in the room. Their wax hands clapping upon each other, as well as the jaded luminosity filming their real eyes, attested to this. How proud and happy I felt.

"Julie," Gerard addressed me, "I've been waiting for you."

"But you're a married man," I protested, hearing gentle laughter from Sir Phalatrope.

The laughter increased and multiplied until I picked up the clue.

"So much the better," I said. "I will meet you later, as scheduled." It had been the correct remark. The jeering stopped and was replaced by nods of approval from many paraffin heads.

I was glad to be of service. I tucked the money underneath my breasts with a toss of my blonde hair. Concentrating on my services and appearance, as well as on how much money I was making, I was able to forget Joseph. I never thought of the deserted room upstairs, or worried about the assignments of Madelaine. Time had never passed as quickly. And though I ached from the twelve-inch heels, and from clutching the feather with my sphincter, I felt calmer.

It seemed minutes later, but hours had passed when the music stopped. Sir Phalatrope turned the bright lights on. In this light the girls looked tired. Judging from their pallor, many were surviving on and being destroyed by amphetamines. Some had occasional spasms from overdoses of Doriden that had begun to deaden parts of their nervous systems. Perspiration darkened the fuchsia. It ran in lines down their sides from beneath the armpits. Food stains were plainly visible.

I saw that Florence's heavy net stockings had been mended again and again with coarse black thread. Her fuchsia shoes revealed dark spots where the dye had worn off.

"Who is to be sacrificed tonight?" asked Joseph, speaking into a microphone from the center of the room.

My eye caught the gleam of Sir Phalatrope's green ring and I nearly fainted. He held me against his stiff jacket, thus shielding my view.

"I must see."

"Fee blue so eager du gleapedog ble fleebunsnon?" he asked.

"Yes," I answered, watching Joseph as he removed his tie, shirt and striped jacket. He put on a lilac apron. I trembled and stared at my cold empty hands. The others sat quietly, limbs hanging rigid from enormous doses of Thorazine. We watched bravely, clutching our plumage. Dark bands of perspiration moved swiftly down the sides of our costumes.

Some of the men still ate or wiped their upper moustaches and lips with the red dinner napkins. They glanced up occasionally between artful chess movements. And all this time, Gerard was behind the cash register counting what had come in. I watched his lips moving as he lay the twenty-dollar bills in a separate pile. Sir Phalatrope looked over his shoulder to see that no error was made in his calculation.

He dismembered her as a French chef dismembers a duck. The joints were cut cleanly and no one piece adhered to another. He knew where the right ligaments were, and how to avoid hitting bones or causing too much blood to spurt.

Then he cleaned up. Gerard took the final total. Sir Phalatrope wiped his forehead with his black handkerchief. We stapled our food order cards together and stuck them on a shelf near the derby. From a large drawer in the walnut cabinet we took our money which we had transferred from beneath our breasts into numbered jars. No one spoke. Florence watched me in silence, her eyes fluttering spasmodically. When I remembered Gerard, and what Madelaine had assigned, I could not look at her again.

After undressing in the crowded dressing room and hanging my costume on a numbered hook, I began searching for the stairway leading to Joseph's room. The kind Sir Phalatrope had waited for me. He led me through the darkness with a blue ship's lantern. I made my way upstairs with his footsteps behind me. "Gleam blue sedation?" he asked. I shook my head negatively as he reached above me to open the floor panel. He helped me to climb into the room. Then he left through the door inside the empty closet.

Once again the change in the room assaulted me. There were no yellow rugs, amber lamps, or art history books. The remains of the cat had disappeared. The bed covered with a gray blanket, a small bureau, and maroon drapes were the room's sole objects.

I stood in the center of the room over the closed floor panel for a long while. Then I noticed the pointed shoes beneath the maroon drape. I shuddered as Madelaine came from the false window. I wondered how long she had been waiting for me, and if Sir Phalatrope had arranged it.

Dressed in black satin, her fleshy face almost hiding her gray eyes, she smiled at me with pointed teeth that were not real. Then she put on her glassless spectacles and peered at me.

"Follow me," she said, hypnotizing me with her voice and with the bursts of light that jumped from her arm. It was braceleted with hand-tooled silver snakes possessing eyes of ruby. Minute diamonds refracted light beneath the shadow of each scale. Around and around her fleshy arm they wound, glittering with tempting blood-drenched eyes. One hundred minute silver snakes criss-crossed in a never ending chain, disappearing beneath her satin sleeve. I followed.

As the escalator made its slow ascent to the first level where I knew Gerard would be waiting, she stood two steps above me, her dyed red hair wilting and crackling along her black satin shoulders. She stood apart from me, but it was as though her hand held mine. And as we traveled upward, I could not guess if she smiled lewdly or if she diffidently studied an obscure map.

Once off the escalator, she led me to a closed white door with a huge clock above it. It was well past midnight, but I felt no fatigue. The pains from my labor below had vanished. One thing surely had nothing to do with another. Not even closely connected segments of time. It was best, then, to let time fall into fresh segments, whether separated by sleep, by a new mental fascination, or by a moving stairway which had always existed, though never as poignantly as now. (I. TAKE GERARD FROM FLORENCE.)

Thus, with foreboding that was fresh, I entered the room. Madelaine waited, in black and silver, against the wall outside the door.

Gerard was passive as a young girl, his body undressed, looking backward and forward in time. I did not try to reach him. We performed, as we would in the many nights to come, with minimal desire. If fingers can be both eager and dead, his were. I accepted everything. Madelaine had triumphed. His wheezing and trembling did not stop us, nor did an echo of Florence, crying in some distant corner of the house, cause us to hesitate in our love ritual.

I emerged with Gerard, although we turned in different directions—he toward a shadowed alcove and I toward Madelaine, who waited with a faint smile lighting up her dry skin.

My reserve was exhausted. I needed familiarity. I wanted to rest in my room with Joseph and to be fed apricot brandy beneath warm lamps. But that Joseph no longer existed, nor did that room. She led me further. I do not think it was wise of her to gamble so much in one night. But once Madelaine began, she was afraid to stop. I needed to sleep, but instead we continued our ascent on the escalator. We rode miles upward and exited into a tower I had always known would be there. It was here that

Madelaine did her work; not in the room she shared with the magician. The precise nature of her work was revealed to no one. She worked and planned way inside this cylinder late into the night and on the days that we did not catch a glimpse of her.

In the center of the room was the drawing board where she worked long hours preparing intricate maps which only she knew how to decipher. She also worked on large charts that were related to the stars. She laughed to herself up here, as she devised subtle strategies to assure at least partial surrender.

"This is the only place where I can think clearly," she said, without looking at me. "I can see the entire view of the house, including the door," she said, picking up a pair of powerful spy glasses.

Alfred and Hannah were gagged and tied together, back to back. Madelaine laughed when she saw me studying them.

"I only tie them up when they get in my way. Otherwise they amuse me as cats would amuse others. I've never been fond of cats."

"Did you decapitate Joseph's cat?" I asked. But she pretended not to hear me. She began tracing maps that were scattered over her drawing board. As she worked, her pointed shoes with silver filigreed buckles swung back and forth underneath the elevated table. After a few moments of concentration, she glanced at Alfred and Hannah.

"I just let them go on as they would if they were alone." She untied them and they thanked her. She returned to the high stool and continued drawing.

"Who is she?" asked Alfred, regarding me.

"To be sure, I never saw her before," said Hannah.

"They are lying," I said to the back of Madelaine.

Madelaine laughed.

"Please let me recite a poem," begged Hannah. We all applauded this suggestion as was the custom. Even I, despite my anger at their refusal to recognize me, joined in. It felt familiar and reassuring to hear Hannah reading a poem as she used to in the green corridor or at our dinner table. Because they had been absent from our banquets for so long, we had surmised that Alfred and Hannah had eloped.

> Under tether
> Up the river
> Gange, Yangtze I have wandered
> Finding lovers with their partners
> Kissing, wading then exchanging
> Cats for rats and rats for pigs
> Night for day and end for in
> She for me and he for him.
>
> Moonlight over splattered kisses
> Sediment of Spermwood sung in Gange.
>
> There I wander in the moonlight
> On the treadle I am winding
> From the boats to water blinding
> Naked statues seen in windows
> Rowing by the river Yangtze

I don't know where I have wandered.

"That's very nice, Hannah," said Madelaine with warmth.

Hannah looked shyly at her husband Alfred.

"Now pass the marmalade, duck," he screamed and began chasing me about the circular tower. Hannah hardly noticed, so overwhelmed with her poem was she.

Madelaine chuckled. "They usually copulate about now. But I think you've upset Alfred."

"One less teacher equals one more grapefruit, marmalade, less a duck, twenty rubber bands. Swine. Haven't I given you ten chances to subdue your children and clean the classroom. You must be done away with lest my entire edifice crumble. Destroy pollutants. Click, click, one two three, five apples take away five."

He began to hit me on the head with one of Madelaine's steel rulers.

"Kill the duck. Kill the duck," he shouted as blood streamed down my forehead. I felt no pain.

Madelaine slid off her high stool. "It's you or him." She stated simply the rule of war. Then she smiled with maternal condescension upon the scene that she had created. With a slightly pontifical silence, she left the tower. I heard her key as she locked us inside. Desperately I called Joseph, Gerard, and Sir Phalatrope. I tapped the wall for secret exits. But there was no way to leave. And the others, even if they would have come, were miles below. They swept the club room, disposed of the body, or slept in their rooms off the green corridor.

"Hannah," I pleaded, "please tell Alfred not to murder me."

"Hurts a bit where I sit," she replied sleepily. And embracing the symbol of copulation she closed her eyes. From her smile I saw that she dreamed peacefully.

For a long time I lay on my back, hands over my eyes letting Alfred beat me with the silver bar.

Hours passed before I realized that I was not going to be rescued. Madelaine would not return in time, as I hoped, and announce that it was a big joke. Nor would Hannah awaken suddenly and comprehend the evil taking place around her.

When I discovered that I was weakened by the current of blood spurting from my temple, I began to see the words 2. MUR-DER ALFRED printed on the wall, ceiling, and inside my head. Although I had protested, it was the thing I wanted to do. It made no difference whether or not he had beaten me. I would have murdered him in any case. I had known this yesterday. I knew it now. I had reasons. Had he not deprived me of my children, and of my position in P.S. X? I had been jailed for vandalism, beaten for lateness, and humiliated in front of the entire teaching community for passing notes.

As he sat back to survey his work, I picked up the bristly rope that Madelaine used to tie them together. It was simple to slip it around his neck as he bent over me. With waning strength I pulled it tighter in small jerky movements. He was so intent upon the massacre of my temple, that he did not notice my counter assault. The light from the silver bar had hypnotized him. He went on and on until with a futile gasp he let it fall from his hand. He never knew what happened. He fell back and turned blue instantly. Hannah awoke and covered him. Soon Madelaine returned. She picked me up into her arms and carried me out of the tower for first aid. She kissed me gently because of my obedience. I slept peacefully, not caring to fight her will any longer.

"You are as bad as the rest of us," she whispered. And it comforted me to hear it. I was very tired.

—

Breakfast was peaceful. Joseph presided with dignity and tact. He spoke of how efficiently we had done our household tasks. Florence was welcomed back from the isolation room. And we were informed that her mother was in the infirmary recuperating from an attack of colitis.

Joseph, assuming an air of ingenuousness, patted me on my bandaged head and asked if I felt better this morning. His question enraged me. Had I not worked effectually in the club below, and committed Madelaine's assignments with grace? Did he secretly object? But it was he, not I, who had abandoned the amber room and left me prey to her whims.

Sir Phalatrope and Joseph whispered about me with concern. Had I made a terrible mistake in answering Florence's call and abandoning the robe that Joseph had given to me when we were lovers? Or had I failed to serve the clients properly?

I ate breakfast in silence, conscious of their secret stares and certain that I had made some serious error that would have even worse repercussions. I must remember to be more cautious, not to answer everyone's bidding, I thought. First I should examine their documents: passport, driver's license, proof of birth, death, and marriage certificate. Some men, for example, came singularly. That could be proven within a reasonable doubt. But the others had a female hidden beneath a flowered quilt with one eye open. Or wide awake writing a short story in the midst of the deception. She was hidden behind a mountain, down a side road in an alcoholics' hospital or mental institution. There is no end to the disguises of existing wives, I thought. For example, Gerard. It appeared that he was not alone. But I could not be sure just when this happened or if it was about to terminate. Nor was I certain that Florence had any part in it. Perhaps I was Gerard's wife. This was no more or less possible than anything else. I must be careful about these things.

I made up my mind to explore, with care, the documents of each person in Madelaine's house. I did not exclude Sir Phalatrope, for he could be an impostor as well. From now on I would believe nothing that was told to me. I would request documentation and evidence.

"In this way I will make fewer mistakes." I spoke this sentence aloud, forgetting that they were watching every move I made. (Secretly I was waiting for Alfred Blatt to appear.) Besides, the others were armed with indices of various sorts; file cabinets, loose-leaf books, and green-inked cards. Even Florence carried a small book into which she put wise sayings that would help her later. (I will keep a notebook with secret observations and conclusions.)

It was a long day in the corridor. I marked it on my calendar. Sir Phalatrope whispered to me that leaves were falling on the white horse. It made me happy.

Later, Florence's mother returned from the infirmary, wearing her filthy turquoise shift. She did not speak or order me to change the water in the pansy cups. She twisted her hair between her thumb and third finger while gazing at the wall. Others gossiped about Hannah and Alfred. It had been rumored for days that they were planning to elope after carrying on for some time in an unorthodox and irreverent manner. It was thought that their disappearance meant a logical consummation of the affair. Besides, many green-inked cards were lying about or crumpled up in the waste paper basket. I picked them up one by one and inspected them, looking for a clue. (I hoped I hadn't murdered him.)

Despite their stares, which had initially made me uncomfortable, I was now confident. Once having come to terms with the fact that, due to Madelaine, I had made a mistake, I awaited the opportunity to inspect documents. Then I might rectify my error.

Daylight provided me with no clues to my relationships with the people in the house. And their behavior had become less predictable than before. In fact no one could be counted upon to make his appearance at breakfast or dinner twice consecutively. However, as I often marveled, the table was always set meticulously for nine. Since the elopement of Hannah with my principal, Mr. Blatt, the meals were silent. Sir Phalatrope came late and gave his benediction to whomever was seated. About once a week Madelaine was present with eyes less veiled; clearer and more vehement beneath pockets of glowing flesh. She wore the same gown no matter what the hour and carried a beaded drawstring purse full of mimeographed maps.

What carried me past these long days, when I realized that nowhere was anything as it had been, and when I was not certain what terrible things I had done, was the vision of my occupation in the club below.

For many days I depended upon night as a time of definition. I awaited impatiently the red glow beneath, where all activity was circumscribed. One sensed a hierarchy. And those people for whom I searched during the day and could not find would be there; Gerard tending the bar, Florence working by my side in the identical costume, Joseph performing the sacrifice, and Sir Phalatrope watching over us with patience.

In that setting, free of Madelaine, just as Florence was free of her mother, I did not have to wrestle with values and action. The adaptations were pleasureful at the outset. I could rest my mind and perceive the stinging of my coarse net stockings with pleasure. (Free, I thought, I was free of Madelaine.)

THE EROTIC MANUAL

Through time, the intensity of our lives diminished. Sometimes, mercifully, my vision was less acute. A mist, neither neutral nor noxious, bathed the personalities surrounding me. This temporary glaucoma subdued the colors of my nightmares and made the viciousness of Madelaine benign: the snake eyes did not glitter. Between relapses, when the sizes of objects changed, and each color split into microscopic skeins, I had respite.

Memory, too, had lost its violence. It made me only vaguely sad to recall the joy I had known with Joseph when we first touched each other. And the gentle orgasms that came before he undressed me; the realization of his presence had released that much rapture. He had wanted to give me everything then. This Joseph, murderer of women, whose crime was an art of perfect craftsmanship. I could not remember the smell of his beard with certainty or the specific gentleness of his fingers.

Long ago I had welcomed Gerard into my bed, not caring to whom he belonged or that I was mechanically obeying Madelaine. Gerard made love to me as though he, too, was simply echoing a principle of hers. Or of his own. We were meticulous. After an energetic performance he left. (The nights varied only slightly.) I do not know whether, subsequently, he roamed the empty cellars that smelled faintly of blood from the nightly slaughter, or if he returned to Florence.

Gerard was becoming thinner and had developed, in addition

to his asthma, a hyperactive thyroid condition with accompanying sweat and bodily tremor. Of all of us, he was most aware of what was happening. He was perplexed by his lack of control over these events, and confessed to me that he was uneasy, wondering who was being hurt by our affair. And he worried about the kidnapping of Hannah and Alfred. (The theory that they had eloped had long been abandoned because of secret evidence possessed by Madelaine which she was unwilling to share.)

Gerard blamed himself for my presence in the house. He admitted his conspiratorial relationship with Madelaine. At her bidding he had followed me to literary convocations and into the bars of disreputable hotels. She had, according to Gerard, a need to possess me that was composed of love as well as of a desire to totally destroy me.

It was then that I understood her hesitations, sudden kisses, and the moments she regarded me with pity.

Gerard had fallen in love with Florence while nursing an unrequited passion for me. Thus he had become avid in his desire to have both of us powerless in this house. Drunk with importance (for he and Madelaine had planned the initial steps behind the firs), he dreamed, in the circular tower, of further conquests and acquisitions.

Madelaine had believed him rational enough to save her in those moments when frenzy would otherwise lead her to self-defeating activity. Inevitably she discovered his vulnerability. Knowing the dangers inherent in an insatiable lust for power, she abandoned him. But he admitted that he still had hopes of ingratiating himself once again.

What made Gerard's position difficult was its uncertainty; it suited their purposes to keep him in a constant condition of fluctuation. From the duties assigned him he attempted to gather clues. But it was useless. When he was commissioned to work by the side of the distinguished Sir Phalatrope, he believed himself at the apex of the hierarchy. But in reality, Sir Phalatrope and

Madelaine made the essential plans alone. At least this is what Gerard surmised. Their intimate relationship he would not disclose, even if he knew.

(But I never lost faith in the magician. I knew that he had an answer for me.)

Notwithstanding the subdued nature of our feelings, an affection grew between Gerard and me. It was nothing like the passion I had shared with Joseph. Perhaps it was the mutuality of our betrayal of Florence and the admission of guilt and guiltlessness at once, that colored the dispassion of our love with empathy.

Gerard would not tell me everything. He did not let me know the nature of his relationship with Joseph. Or if he saw Florence any more. He warned me, however, that in the weeks to come, my duties in the club below might become more than I could tolerate.

"In that case you will be put in solitary confinement."

I understood only too well. And I resolved to serve my clients impeccably. For despite sluggishness and inaccuracies resulting from barbiturates, I knew that the foul-smelling cavern below was closer to Sir Phalatrope's horse than was the isolation room off to left center of the green corridor. I made the choice and tried to live up to it, as Florence must have done before me.

—

Although we were little more than puppets, we were at least acknowledged as part of the existing society. As for the autonomy of thought, as it could exist in isolation. Were those thoughts so vital? Or was that individuality we clung to, using signposts such as turquoise robes and glittering boundary lines, just as arbitrary and inessential as the maps of Madelaine?

Bravely we abandoned our carefully constructed selves and went behind the stairwell. In this spot, where Sir Phalatrope waited, was an archway covered with black velvet curtains. Two girls led the way by candlelight, as we escorted our clients into small rooms that were bare but for huge canopied Victorian beds and mirrored ceilings.

At a sudden whim, trays and food orders were forgotten. In fact we were urged to await their most fleeting impulse, and react instantly. It was fanned carefully until it took the form of a desire. Once inside the room, the desire would be skillfully enlarged, made specific and fulfilled.

I made many serious mistakes. I did not understand the restraint required of art. I dissipated my energies, imagining that each man was my awaited love. To each my arms were open. Regardless of his age or disposition, I saw him as my personal Adam come at last to insulate my garden. Thus my performances were sincere and impassioned. I soon learned from Florence of the complaints filed against me. I was too avid. My sentimentality was grotesque. The expansive gestures that I made were vulgar. And I lacked subtlety.

It was not passion that was desired, I learned, but a sip of some powerful distillate served sparingly in a lavish glass.

Joseph reprimanded me harshly, trapping me in a corner as I emerged from the velvet curtain followed by an angry customer. "Annihilate your emotionality. Destroy all remains of craving. Be moderate in giving. Avoid personal exchange. Use yourself as a pure erotic instrument." He handed me a training manual. Though it was a sign of my failure, I studied it gratefully.

Instinctively I realized that my survival depended upon its mastery. In addition to the chapters on gesture, technique, posturing, and correct attire, there was a section on the science of non-involvement. It was over the latter that I labored most assiduously. It was hard to recondition myself. But I was pleased to know, at last, what was really desired.

As a symbol of my growing insight, I threw away my pink garter belt trimmed with rosebuds and black lace. Instead, I placed, just below my hips, a narrow band of leather. The garter hooks were covered with authentic alligator skin. Microscopic needles jingled from each band. Later I painted my nipples white. My lips were also white, and these white shapes were delineated with artful blue lines.

With each object designed for specific purposes I moved further from habitual thought patterns. In a small metallic case I carried my equipment. There were black eye masks, geometrically shaped, thin silver links, vinyl nipple caps, snakeskin gloves with several fingers removed, simple thigh belts, cords, feathers, and delicate whips. Joseph was pleased.

"You are learning," he said.

The first principles that I discovered were the most significant for my transformation. Least did they want anything that reminded them of affection. Or of self. It was to annihilate the self through pure erotic experience that they came to me. To create the most intense erotic shocks it was necessary to become anonymous.

I began to see what Gerard's warning had implied. To achieve the desired end, I had to expel the most basic part of my individual proclivity. A moody sexuality clung to me despite my effort. I worked for months to change my sexual tone. I depersonalized myself as much as was possible and extracted a purely erotic self that I had not known existed. But I still had a major flaw. This was a desire to please. It made my movements exaggerated, my efforts painful, my performance less polished. It was out of place. Joseph often followed me into the Victorian bed to test me.

"You are still too intent. Intensity has no place in pure sexuality."

He taught me the details that would make my work "professional." A method for eroticizing any portion of the body was demonstrated. A circular skin clamp was used to isolate this area. It then became a matter of concentration, timed display, and covering, as well as prohibition and invitation. I enjoyed learning. It took my mind from its usual preoccupation with past and future. Joseph was an exacting instructor. He wanted my philosophical position to be clear to me. And he was always on guard to prevent my exhausted psyche from resorting to bitterness or self-pity.

"Accept the reality of human sexuality," he repeated. "Accommodate your behavior to this. Destroy romantic fantasies at once. But do not destroy your basic sex drive."

"He does not want you to become frigid," whispered Florence.

He did not want me to lose my feminine instincts, but he insisted that I destroy my sentimentality and replace it with intellect and imagination.

"Within the limits I have prescribed, I want you to achieve total control of your thoughts and of the behavior of your body."

I studied very hard and asked millions of questions. Gerard, passing in the distance, or descending into the cellar universe, observed what was going on with a worried glance.

"She will never survive," I heard him whisper to Sir Phalatrope, who was leaning on the walnut cabinet where we kept the numbered jars. The latter smiled with great wisdom and sorrow while motioning for Gerard to go about his business.

But I was surviving, and learning to accept the sexual situation unemotionally, according to its own terms. I accepted the variations in male sexuality, and its dire extremes, as I would accept variations in the way they walked or what they desired for breakfast. Nor did I request their love, even silently.

I gave willingly. But it was through the art of my erotically oriented techniques and never with my emotions. With total disengagement I cured the impotent and caused committed homosexuals to respond. So scientific was Joseph's art and so adept had I become in its practice that it never failed.

Florence was also becoming less vulnerable to men through her practice of the new art. I watched as she conducted client after client through the curtains. (It was like watching myself in a mirror.) She emerged refreshed rather than enervated. There was never a longing glance after the man, no matter how fascinating he appeared. A tear never fell down her cheek. Even when Gerard followed her, and emerged after a brief interval, she was as before; ostrich feather in rectum, walking smoothly with her head held high. I saw that there was more dignity to this than to the yearning and longing for Gerard's arms that had precipitated her entrance into the house.

"We are improving," I whispered to her one evening as we passed each other.

"I hope so," she said with some caution. Then she also warned me of the tests to come. But I did not realize how close I was, if I failed, to a final place in the green corridor.

The nights passed, one like the other. I received only praise from Joseph (as well as a smile from Sir Phalatrope), to congratulate my performance.

———

November eighth I escorted a handsome young man into my bed. (Earlier, Joseph had demonstrated a new combination using the basic thigh cord movement with laryngeal acoustics.) It required extraordinary concentration to create the exact tone at the instant that the cord began to roll. The challenge was great and I was anxious to employ this technique with my customer. To my amazement he tore off the cords as well as my shoulder clamps. Then he slowly removed my hexagonal eye coverings, breast clippers, red mesh, boned corset, and toe pads.

"It is against the rules to be entirely naked," I protested, fearing Joseph's reprimand. But he did not stop until I was completely undressed. Only then did he express a long-frustrated passion for me. He spoke of seeing me before, in places outside this house: in gardens, waiting on train platforms, in libraries, museums, and at literary teas.

As he spoke he held me very gently. Occasionally he kissed my cheek or held my breasts in his hand. I listened. When he made love to me it was with the combination of sensitivity and passion that I used to dream of in those days before the end of dreaming. "There is love," he said. Then he promised to prove it by leading me from the false night in which I lived.

My dehumanization vanished. I forgot the arduous months of labor and the discipline that had created from my excessive desire, a perfect erotic instrument. My lover resuscitated the longing that Joseph had sought to destroy. I regressed to the emotional passion I had known before; and beyond. Tears came from my eyes and extraneous unrehearsed sounds from my mouth. As hour after hour disappeared, I forgot the mirrored ceiling, Victorian bed, as well as my obligations in the main room.

I lay back against his shoulder dreaming of the day he would return and take me past the corridor to the gate outside. He dreamed too, I thought. But when he turned toward me his eyes were opaque. They reflected me like disengaged mirrors.

"You did very well," he said, extracting a small tape recorder from beneath the mattress. He played back to me the record of our past hours. As I listened without breathing, he laughed. He laughed hardest at the submissive responses I had made to his slightest intimation of affection. The tape continued as he buttoned his shirt and fastened the metallic clasp above his zipper. Then he laced his shoes slowly, while glancing at me with a derisive smile.

"Did everything go well?" Joseph asked from the vestibule outside.

"Excellently," responded my lover, putting the tape recorder underneath his arm. I began to tremble violently. As he turned to leave, without a good-bye, I screamed and threw myself on the floor in a condition of mild seizure. Then I beat him with my fists while he laughed.

Joseph entered. He slapped my face and led me upstairs to our empty room off the green corridor.

For days I screamed. I trembled and saw black angels on the wall. I lost all control over the sizes of objects in the room. Sometimes I cowered in the corner, afraid to move, nibbling absently at the food that Sir Phalatrope brought to me. Other times I beat the walls with my fists until they tied my arms to the bed. Time was lost, as was the line between sleeping and waking. There were dreams induced by many drugs. I saw mice crawling up the walls, and when they reached the top I put a piece of bristly rope around their necks and pulled in weak jerks, again and again, until they fell to the ground.

At last the magician came in purple robes and sat at the edge of my bed. He reminded me that the horse was still waiting for the journey. Gently he persuaded me to try again; he convinced me that I had almost succeeded.

"But each fall is worse than the one before," I said.

"Yes," he answered sadly, stroking my hand.

But this in itself was of no importance. I knew it would not happen again. Until I was far away on the magic horse I would become an instrument, deaf to my own emotions. Hadn't I proof of their random destructive nature? Hadn't I witnessed feelings tyrannize me? It was going to be harder this time, because I no longer had any hope.

It took weeks for the angels to disappear from the walls and for the objects to become clear once more. No longer did the colors frighten me nor did the motions of cats cause me to hide my eyes. Can I thank Sir Phalatrope for recognizing me even then? And for understanding that it was best to promise me nothing?

I know that hidden in the closets of all amber rooms are growling impatient cats. I see the shadow of their legs beneath the bathroom door and sense their growing restlessness. And while I lie back in a trance they are getting ready to claw through the wood and kill me. I do not know why this has to be so. Sir Phalatrope, the magician, did not explain it to me. In silence he communicated to me that he knew it was so; that the assaults were real. He could trace the black angel on the wall at the moment it appeared. Then he looked at me and made me smile. And though I no longer sought advice or love, I did want to understand the meaning of my existence in this house. If I ever left, with whom would I go?

———

I was not permitted to go downstairs in search of Joseph or Gerard. Instead I did simple tasks. She did not have to ask me to change the water. I awaited the end of each interval impatiently and handled the pansies with care. I swept the floor and set the table, and when the others disappeared at dusk, I searched their rooms for documents. Sir Phalatrope disapproved. He laughed and shook his head, but he allowed me to see everything.

"Do blue really care what peenin fleebunnon themselves to glive?" he asked sadly. "Or du flupe they are lifed?"

It was then I realized that he was very old. I hadn't noticed it, long ago, when he came through my closet presenting me with a photograph of the house as it may have been or never was. He had been agile and full of mischief crawling from beneath glittering cloth. He wasn't like that any more. His movements were slower and his laugh was full of hesitation. More often he smiled sadly. He was majestic but sometimes I feared he had lost his gon blye white horse. I loved him very much. But I still cared what people were called and whether they lived alone or with a wife. I wanted to know about the work they performed and the degree of their dedication. Greedily I tore at the documents—stole and memorized them. To reassure myself, I recited what I had memorized before I fell asleep.

My own documents, real or falsified, had been stolen. I found in their place a mimeographed letter with an abbreviated map. It read:

Elaine. It is time to confront Joseph. Time is dissolving. Hurry. Follow paths G, Q, and M. Then circle forth where the line meets the green cross. Advance with caution.

The words "Confront Joseph" puzzled me. Was I to accuse him? If so, what was his crime? Oh yes, desertion. That was one. (I spoke aloud.) "At liberty. Murder. Betrayal. False identification. Insufficient food. Outdated methods. Innuendo. Indecent exposure. Polygamy. Lasciviousness. Betrayal of the Hippocratic Oath." His violations were endless when one began to count them. Well fortified, I sought him.

Advancing with caution, as directed, I came to the half-opened door of the isolation room. Pale and trembling, he was whittling small figures of women with a gilt-edged paring knife. I was shocked. It was the first time I had seen Joseph when he was unaware of the presence of others. He whittled at a pace so rapid I could barely follow his movements. Perspiration formed small puddles at his feet. And countless configurations of wood floated within. On the back of an ordinary chair hung his striped jacket. It was stained with food and covered with sawdust. Lilac aprons spattered with blood were thrown carelessly around the small room. All was incredible disorder. Joseph sat on an unmade bed among the random twisting and turning of sheets, completely possessed.

I pushed back the door. Then, after closing it silently, I sat on a chair facing him. Madelaine's mimeographed letter was in my hand.

"I cannot stop," he said. Figures formed an arc around him. I picked up one and examined it, discovering that it was a small reproduction of one of the fuchsia-clad girls below.

"There is a motor inside. Push the button beneath her hair."

I did, and she began to writhe, gyrate, and kick up her leg swathed in red net.

"Watch," he said. "Here is the man."

He pulled from beneath his bed three sides of a box lined with mirrors. He attached mirrored floors and ceilings so that the women grouped around him (or the replica of himself) could be viewed from additional angles.

"Pornography is my life and art," he said. "The female body surrounds him wherever he looks. Now I press the buttons. His head moves and they dance. Lovely erotic machinery above, below, everywhere. It must continue. It must surround him, exciting him, rousing him forever."

I observed the fluttering. Up and down. Too weak to sustain itself. Too nervous to relax. He took it in his hand.

"It didn't happen at once. No. Very slowly I detached myself from any other relationship to it . . . her. First it was a diversion. Then a passion. Now it is an obsession. One body. Another. It is never enough. Constant exploration is a necessity. Otherwise I am not certain. I am not certain that I am alive."

It fluttered again. He grabbed it, but it collapsed.

The fourth mirrored wall was added, after removing a small fragment, through which he could see. He stared into it breathing rapidly. My presence was forgotten. Whether or not I existed as a wooden figurette was no longer any concern of mine. I assumed that my motors were as carefully installed as the others. And that my leg kicked as high.

Hours passed as he watched, shaking with excitement among the twisted sheets. The gilt-edged paring knife was clenched in his fist.

"It is not enough," he said, with a sudden movement away from his toy. "Each day it needs more room for expression. I would like the entire world to resemble a chaotic design of interpenetrating mirrors. I would stand at the center as they reflect and refract an infinitesimal mirage of erotic machinery. Females upside down. Entwined. Inviting. Withdrawing. Half-children. Women. Half-men. Constantly gathering momentum. Disappearing only to tantalize and then display themselves in strange mutations . . . full of electricity. Or totally inert. My body aches. I cannot eat or sleep. My mind is always working out new designs."

"Have you become impotent yet?" I asked with the cruel marksmanship of Madelaine.

His hand released its hold in a sudden spasm. The knife slipped and he stared at the fluttering remains.

I laughed then, Madelaine's husky laugh. And Joseph diminished in size. Afraid to look at me, he held his head in his hands and sobbed. Stealthily I took a matchbox from beneath one of my tiny breasts. With loud friction along the center it broke into a flaring torch. I burned the wooden man and his world. Then, full of triumph and guilt, I stumbled out of the isolation room. Joseph remained; irrational among crusted sheets, charred wood, and melting wax. Nothing fluttered.

"You have destroyed Joseph," said Madelaine, who was waiting outside the door beneath the clock which moved as she willed. She made a big red check on her copy of my assignment sheet.

"You did not escape me," she said, searching my face to make certain. Opening her beaded drawstring purse, she took out the coiled silver snake bracelet, and handed it to me. Without hesitation, I let it wind around my arm. I stared into her eyes; Madelaine of my dreams, of the death that clung to me since I first recognized her power over my mind.

Since my first submission, at the end of an escalator, I had gradually stopped fighting her will. But I had been afraid. It was only now that my fear of her disappeared. I let her become part of me as she always had demanded. And I accepted the fusion.

I cried too, as I saw the remains of my destruction; Joseph staggering with his arm resting on Sir Phalatrope's maroon cape. They were receding slowly down the corridor. The magician, feeling my gaze, turned around and waved. Still weeping, Madelaine and I returned his greeting.

PART TWO

To say that I ever left the house would be a lie. Just as it was a distortion to say that I entered it at some precise moment. There are really no doors or gates leading in or out of that house. Of course one can be coerced or ignored. One can avoid the engagement and escape into something else. But those technicalities are of no importance. They are just illusions, in the same sense that birth and marriage certificates are; they serve their function for society. For the individual, the value and meaning of these documents is subjective; release as a permanent fact is just a mirage.

The house was always changing; it always will be changing, as will be my view of it.

—

Soon after I fulfilled her requirements and accepted the predatory bracelet, Madelaine departed. Perhaps she was hidden somewhere, observing from behind the firs. I doubt it. My sense of her as a specific being was lost. Her departure, however, was not absolute. Evenings, when there was nothing to do, I often played dominoes with her carcass; a woman whose favorite attire was a black taffeta dress which swished even as she crossed her legs. She too carried a beaded drawstring purse. But rather than maps, this purse contained letters from people who had stopped writing, crumpled tissues, and pieces of rock candy on a filthy string that she liked to suck. That she always managed to draw the double six and lead off no longer bothered me, nor did her excessive glee when inevitably I was defeated. Call her Madelaine, call her anything; she was not my Madelaine, not even in my dreams.

This Mrs. Gilligan was fascinated by the occult. And in certain moods she became rambunctious, proclaiming her ability to control the fate of everyone in the house. She also swore that she could make plates float and tables levitate at will. In her room she kept various astrological charts. I think she invented them without any help from the stars. In addition was an ordinary paperweight that she called her crystal ball. Sir Phalatrope, the magician, humored her and spent what seemed an excessive number of hours in her room. I heard them talking and laughing at bizarre, incredible hours, but I could not imagine that he, a true magician, could take her nonsense seriously.

I myself was becoming disappointed in Sir Phalatrope. For one thing he no longer came through my closet to visit but knocked on the door like anyone else. Nor did he wear his cape lined with gold dust. I assumed that he had his reasons. But it disturbed me. I had counted upon him too strongly, I suppose. And when he came to talk to me in an ordinary suit jacket—still the cuffless trousers and striped socks—I lost faith in his power to help. In fact I told him so and carried on quite a bit about it. When he protested that he was just an ordinary man, I threatened not to let him inside my room at all. He laughed. I guess he knew that I was lying and would not lose faith in his power no matter what he said or what he wore.

Often he would ask me how I felt about the departure of Madelaine. To which I avoided a direct reply by stating that since he sent her away it was he who should answer that question. I didn't really want an answer, but he always gave me one.

"I bun no gleam for Madelaine."

There was usually a silence after that.

"What do you and Mrs. Gilligan talk about?"

"The stars," he answered, "and what she buns in the flugerf-lup."

"Crystal ball," I corrected, considering it wrong for him to call it a paperweight. He smiled at that.

"Fee blue still afloog of Madelaine?"

I thought that question odd since she was gone and I was wearing the malignant bracelet on my arm. He left me, and though I searched for gold dust on the floor there was none. I cried sometimes because of this. But in my dreams, Sir Phala-trope, wearing a cape, would lead me beyond the firs. Magically, the wooden horse would gallop away.

(Now that Madelaine was gone, her vehemence was mine.)

Evening was still the time I looked forward to. But I no longer followed Joseph's erotic manual as assiduously. I served the par-affin men whose waxed moustaches grew demandingly from hot dilated pores. (However, I sensed that I could easily pull each hair out from its soft bed—and that changed my mood.)

I dressed as carefully, pausing to say a few words to Florence whose eyes blinked and fluttered under the fluorescent tubes.

"I'm glad to see you up and around," she said, referring to my recent disappearance.

I ignored this remark.

"And your mother . . ." I ventured cautiously, as we pulled up the rough-textured stockings and expertly inserted the anus plumes without a grimace.

"I cannot find her," she whimpered, her eyes blinking rapidly and her face twisting spasmodically.

I was momentarily alarmed, but she seemed to recover suffi-ciently to emerge looking exquisite and dignified.

"You forgot your blonde wig," whispered Joseph as I followed.

"I don't need it," I said sharply. He seemed to diminish in size.

"Where is Julie?" asked Gerard, not recognizing me without my blonde wig.

"The wig," exclaimed Sir Phalatrope, Joseph, and Gerard in unison, while the paraffin men laughed derisively.

"I am Elaine," I replied, with the authority of Madelaine, and laughingly beckoned to one of the men who eyed my plumage covetously. He followed me behind the velvet curtains.

I performed well, knowing that Joseph was listening with some anxiety outside. But I no longer trembled at the thought of his reprimand lest I do something not included in the manual. Actually, I did what I had always done, only the concentration, the desire to perfect this erotic art, was absent.

The man emerged, apparently satisfied, but Joseph eyed me with suspicion. I smiled, brushing past him with suggestive laughter, and glided on, waiting on tables and watching for a sign—dilated nostrils, heavy breathing, or glass eyes following the harsh mesh stockings.

Something had changed since Madelaine's departure; even I wasn't sure what it was. Sir Phalatrope watched patiently behind the cash register. He smiled softly when Gerard and Joseph filed a joint complaint against me.

"She is too commanding," I heard Joseph whisper in alarm, and Gerard demanded the blonde-haired Julie.

Not that I had forgotten any of my instructions. I still wore my hexagonal eye coverings and a variety of garter belts that I had designed myself for special effect. My technique was flawless. Joseph conducted me into the Victorian bed to test me.

"I am satisfied on all accounts," he said. "You are uninvolved, you no longer try too hard to please, nor fumble with your specific erotic decisions. You have learned my lessons well."

"So well," I replied, "that I have thrown away your manual. I never practice or rehearse."

A shiver passed over him.

"My manual," he echoed, and having nothing further to say he exited downcast while I smiled at something.

"Why are you smiling?" asked Florence, who met me as I emerged from the room.

"I have discovered something beyond the erotic manual," I replied. But I was not certain what it was, since no overt difference in my work had been discerned by Joseph, the host.

"Be careful," warned Florence. "They suspect something."

Florence, I thought, you will join me when the secret of my own power is revealed to me; then your face will no longer twitch, nor will you be summoning your mother in vain.

—

The nights went on, always changing—but these changes were barely perceptible. One night when the lights went on, Joseph failed to perform the sacrifice. Later, I saw him in a corner of the deserted basement, his pin-striped suit dirty from the cold floor.

"It is your fault I am like this," he sobbed.

I bent to comfort him, but changed my mind and decided to retire to my room.

"Eng what aflooged blue about comforting Joseph?" asked the magician, who was waiting for me with the old ship's lantern.

"Madelaine," I muttered, not certain.

"Yes," he said, without criticism. "But blue bloughten be what you were before; you have gleaped."

I fell asleep dreaming that I held Joseph's hand and then ran into the arms of Sir Phalatrope.

—

Light, disturber of dreams, causing things to emerge too suddenly or to lie waiting in false shadow. Light, destroyer of illusion that comes racing between both eyes before the time is right. How I hated light. I continued to hate it day after day.

Squinting against what I was forced to see, I emerged cautiously from my room. Like a ritual I could not avoid, I bent over the silent deathlike statue of my mother. Her protruding eyes beneath darkened sockets did not look up. Only her fingers moved, twisting a few strands of her thinning hair.

"Mother . . . how are you today? It is I, your daughter Elaine."

There was only the rotary motion of her two thin fingers. I felt my eyes squinting and fluttering, then filling with tears. My small lace handkerchief was soon drenched.

As I wearily retreated to my room, I heard her mocking laughter.

"Daughter indeed," she muttered now and again.

* * *

The table was set as usual for nine. I sat next to Joseph who was trying to make amends for something. My mother and Mrs. Gilligan laughed together as they ate, taking no notice of me. Gerard did not say good morning to anyone. I assumed that he was still angry with me for not wearing the blonde wig. I smiled to myself, remembering that I was no longer the same. Sir Phalatrope had said so.

"Have you a poem to recite?" I asked Hannah.

Everyone looked at me in amazement. Florence put her hands over her ears. And Mrs. Gilligan stopped sucking her rock candies.

"I will speak as loudly as I like," I said, as Sir Phalatrope appeared to see that everything was all right.

"Go ahead, Hannah," he said. And she pulled the poem from inside her brassiere.

> The cocks are bent
> The horse is dead
> I see the feast of flies.
> When he is spent, so quickly spent
> He curls up soft inside.
> Don't die I say
> As he lies still
> Blue and wet and free

The horse's flanks are still alive
And tingle four for thee.
It is the feast of flies.

But that was yesterday.

Today I saw the cocks unfurled
Unbent reach to the sky
And singing ringing scamper
Where the horse lay merrily.
Reach for the sun
And then discharge
Silt and sulphur free.

If it burn mare or she-ass then
She'll still sing merrily.

"Marvelous," said Joseph.

I turned away as Sir Phalatrope congratulated Hannah, who blushed and smiled at the applause.

"It takes a lover to find another," said Alfred Blatt, eyeing Hannah covetously. He ate his toast in small bites, displaying his newly lacquered finger nails.

"Marmalade, my duck," he said suddenly, shifting his glance in my direction.

I shuddered, remembering his assault in the circular tower.

"Cat got your tongue, duck? A word in time saves nine and yards of cards save one. Marmalade, fish or I'll swill your gill."

"I've stolen nothing," I protested. "I swear it. I did the best I could in the kindergarten, Mr. Blatt. If the children ran wild it was no fault of mine. Nor am I concerned with the future reputation of your school."

"Ignore her, Alfred," said my mother with authority.

"I will not be accused any longer," I shouted.

Florence wept nervously as Gerard, dressed in white, came to my defense.

I followed Gerard down the green corridor to his small office. He smiled genially.

"Don't let them bother you," he advised. "I'm hardly appreciated here myself. Of course I can come and go as I please. And I am thinking of leaving. There is better employment elsewhere."

I gasped. "But what about Florence? You promised to marry her."

"Nonsense," he said, smiling. "You know better than that now."

I ran down the corridor, ignoring my mother, whose head was bent over a fresh pile of pansies. Further down I found Florence. She wore a lace veil pinned to her hair and she was humming softly and contentedly to herself.

"Florence," I said, "I must tell you something important."

"Sh . . . sh . . ." she answered, looking beyond me and smiling happily. "Gerard is marrying me tonight," she whispered.

"No, I just spoke to him . . . I must tell you . . ." But she wasn't listening.

It was then, although it could be any time of the day, that I placed my hands over my eyes, too weary to understand. And when I reopened them, everything was changed. It frightened me. For example, at this moment of crisis, I swayed for a moment, then covered my closed eyes. When I opened them I could not imagine what I had wanted to tell poor Florence, who was rocking back and forth in a world of her own. I walked away with a sense of desolation. For what was left me when these moments attacked my dreams so suddenly?

Fortunately, Sir Phalatrope understood. He put into words what I could not.

"The construction you built is falling down. That is good. But it makes you alone and uncomfortable. It is no easy time for you—going back and forth like this."

"Everyone disappears. I have no friend Florence, and no mother."

"Yes, that is painful," he said. "But what about Joseph? Why do you reject his friendship now?"

"Sir Phalatrope, haven't you seen all the terrible things that Joseph has done to me?"

He hesitated. Perhaps he would have said "Yes." But he simply said, "No," and left. No gold dust, no dreams. I wept for many days.

———

Since I wept during the day, and the sudden changes in my own visions exhausted me, I asked the magician if I could stay in my room. He allowed me this respite. It was simply a matter of waiting for the light to fade, for night to surround me again.

During the day I kept the shades drawn and wrote by a small lamp:

Arrest the sunlight and bring back all amber lamps. Open the door so I may leave on the white horse. (I scratched out "white horse.") And may the wedding take place soon.

Much of it makes no sense, but then it made great sense and I wrote with passion. Occasionally Mrs. Gilligan knocked on my door and we played dominoes, or else I let her tell my fortune in her crystal ball.

On the fourth day of my confinement my mother knocked at the door and placed a pansy in a paper cup on my bedside table.

"The actions of people are totally unpredictable," I complained to Sir Phalatrope with some annoyance.

"Yes," he said, "but it does not imply danger."

He left, before I could answer.

———

Forget the days. The nights were as glorious as before. My paradise was below, and I took more and more control of it. I was disappointed to find that Florence was no longer working by my side. I assumed that she had married and that this was not a suitable occupation for a married woman. Gerard appeared and disappeared for many nights.

"Are you leaving?" I asked him as I paraded about the room to the delight of the moustached men who ate and drank, oblivious to Florence's absence.

"I have to make sure that Florence is comfortable," he answered, and I had no time to question him further, since my customers were waiting and Joseph was following my every gesture.

"Would you like to dance?" Joseph asked.

I looked at him in astonishment. "My customers are waiting and I haven't even dressed."

"I see," he said, and reported this transgression to Sir Phalatrope.

"I destroyed the erotic manual," I confessed to the magician, "but my performance has in no way deteriorated."

My clientele grew each night. I was the only remaining waitress. The others had been fired. It seemed logical to me, since I could handle them all in one night and much money could be saved. Out of habit I wore my costume. But there was a growing rebellion within me against its confinement. I complained to Joseph about my aching sphincter and about the rough texture of the mesh stockings.

"But no one ever insisted that you wear them," he lied.

"This is your creation," I screamed at him, "but I will no longer allow you to stamp your methods upon me. From now on I will make my own costumes and create my own erotic philosophy."

He looked hurt and puzzled, but I had not forgotten how he had deserted me, removing himself from our bedroom and using me as a tool for his creations.

"Move aside while I entertain," I commanded.

Respectfully the men stopped eating and folded their false

hands gently in their laps. All glass eyes were turned in my direction. Obligingly, Joseph brought me the microphone. And in my new costume—a white gown with silver swans—I swayed and sang an old torch song. Then I danced, banging a tambourine. They were entranced. Some swooned with delight while others stared, hypnotized.

Joseph brought the props as I demanded them, and Sir Phalatrope applauded. The lights dimmed, and when they came up again the room was deserted. Only Mrs. Gilligan, who had trouble sleeping, sat in the corner playing solitaire and crying over the letters spread over the entire table. Joseph was sweeping the basement floor. Bewildered by the abrupt end to my performance, I sat down to rest before ascending the staircase that led to my room.

THE RING

"Quite a performance," said Joseph, pausing with the broom in his hand. "Everyone enjoyed it."

"Don't judge my performances any more," I warned him.

"But I must, since I'm your doctor," he explained.

Mrs. Gilligan laughed uproariously through her tears.

"He's still playing doctor. And what does the doctor want with the burlesque queen?"

"I'm an artist, not a burlesque queen," I protested indignantly. "What's more important, I have perfected my art and can do whatever I like."

"What are your plans?" asked Joseph with humility.

Mrs. Gilligan, still laughing, was folding up her old letters and putting them into her drawstring purse. She gathered up her playing cards.

"Pleasant dreams," she said as she ascended the steps, her taffeta slips making a swishing sound.

"Oh, I guess I'll open a school eventually. And I will decide the policies," I added, thinking of Mr. Blatt.

"And what will your husband say about that?"

"He will have nothing more to say about anything," I said. "I'm very tired, Joseph. I don't like to stay after the audience has left."

"You're trembling," he said. "I guess it was too soon to mention your husband."

Husband, I thought with alarm, walking around my room. I looked behind the maroon drapes and inside my closet. It took me a long time to open the bottom drawer of my night table. Trembling and wheezing with an impending asthmatic attack, I tried to pull it out. I kicked it. Then I pushed my nail file around the edges; the file broke in two, so I used both halves to pry open the drawer. (Bits of wood shavings floated to the floor, splinters stung my fingertips.) It came out suddenly, crashing to the parquet. Without hesitation I looked inside. My fingers found something covered by wads of tissue—a gold ring. Its gleam attacked me and I collapsed where I had been standing. Dreams assaulted me; Joseph was binding me from head to toe with enormous, crushing gold rings. And he put one inside my mouth to silence me. The table was cold and the stirrups were being pulled further and further apart, until the insides of my legs ached.

I awoke thinking a gold ring was in my eye, but it was only the sun. Gerard, dressed in white, entered with a pleated cup of pills and some breakfast. He urged me to get dressed and wait for Dr. Phalatrope. As I dressed I heard my mother laughing with Mrs. Gilligan.

"I heard that my daughter gave quite a performance last night," she said sarcastically. Joseph raised his voice in anger.

Sir Phalatrope knocked on the door. I opened my mouth to say, "Come in," but no sound emerged. This had happened before, but I could not remember when. I opened the door, pointing at my throat and opening and closing my mouth helplessly. I wanted to say, "husband"; there was no word. I held up the gold ring and threw it on the floor.

"Joseph is very sorry about mentioning your husband," Sir Phalatrope said cautiously. I put my hands over my ears and closed my eyes. Gently he took my hands in his.

"I will talk for you," he said. "You forgot that you have a husband, and you still want to forget. You met him at a gynecological convention and married him a month later. I have had many talks with him and have a fairly clear picture of that year. No, don't pull your hands away. Just listen. He told me about his insistence upon technical excellence in the sexual act, and he explained how he used to test you on your knowledge of the manuals he wrote on the physiology of sex and on the psychology of eroticism. All right, take your hands from mine but don't cover your ears. He has a charming manner and a façade of warmth. But he is afraid of closeness . . . In his own way, and I say this very emphatically, in his own way he loves you. . . ."

"Joseph is not my husband," I shouted, finding my voice in anger.

Sir Phalatrope patted my hand. "No one need be your husband if you don't choose it . . ." Then he left, after urging me to write down my feelings about anyone I cared to. I saw him slip the gold ring into his jacket pocket before he left.

I am not married. Dr. Phalatrope is lying. There are no amber lamps or golden rings. My legs are sore from lying on the gynecological examining table. Joseph cannot force me to accept the gold ring any more.

I slept for a while and awoke to the sound of Florence screaming. I walked from my room into the green corridor.

"Is Florence in labor?" I asked Gerard, who was discussing something with Joseph in low tones. (I remembered Florence telling me that she and Gerard were expecting a child.)

"She seems to think so," answered Gerard coldly.

"And why aren't you with her?" I accused.

"Dr. Phalatrope is with her," he answered. Joseph did not look up.

"Elaine, will you change the water in the pansy cup," commanded my mother from a formica-topped table at the far end of the corridor.

"No, no," I shouted, above the sound of Florence's screaming.

Alfred Blatt looked up from the cards he was arranging beneath the table. "The duck has fouled the water. The thief is nobody's daughter. I'll imprison her before the slaughter, and drown her in bloody water." Slowly he crept closer to me, over the rows of cards, and with a flick of his long white fingers he tossed a card into my lap. It was blank except for the inscription, "foul fowl," and "nobody's daughter."

I wept after reading the card and then tossed it to the center of the floor. I stamped on it with my heel.

"The cards must be in rows," he cried out in alarm. "You have committed the worst crime against the system." He crawled after the card, soiling his custom-tailored pants. Hannah ran to help him as I laughed the vicious laugh of Madelaine.

—

Dinner was silent. Joseph stared at the table and nibbled at his food. My mother had formed a conspiracy with Alfred Blatt and Hannah. They exchanged mocking glances in my direction as I struggled to ignore them. I was too worried about Florence's delivery to be very concerned with the activities around the table. Gerard excused himself early to bring Florence her dinner and Sir Phalatrope arrived looking exhausted.

"Have you a poem this evening?" he asked.

I looked at Hannah and Hannah looked at me. Alfred Blatt snickered and pinched my thigh beneath the table.

"Hannah, your poem," I finally said, rising.

Joseph looked at me for the first time that day. Sir Phalatrope continued to eat his tiny pieces of grapefruit.

> The horse is dead
> In water red
> All wound with rings
>
> And rusty springs.

The owls flew in great alarm
To mourn, lament
The mare lay calm.

How can you lie there, said the ass
And neigh merrily on broken glass
The time is for your stallion's mass.

The mare just laughed rolled merrily.
At last my husband is gone from me
And I can sing and I can play
And chase the cocks this sunny day.

I sat down to the sound of deafening applause.

Only Hannah sat with folded hands. "She wants her poems back," she whispered to my mother in alarm.

"All things must come to an end," said Joseph philosophically. "After all, they're her poems and she has a right to reclaim them."

"But she gave them to me," whined Hannah. "I recited them and it is I who deserve the credit."

"The thief stole Hannah's poems. Get the authorities to burn the duck," said Alfred, squeezing Hannah's hands.

"Let's be just," said Joseph. "Elaine wrote the poems but chose to give them to Hannah. However, it does not change the fact of authorship."

"I cannot agree with your logic," said Alfred. "A gift is an absolute thing, and once given cannot be reclaimed. I say the authorship is Hannah's. What's more, to take back what one has given is the same as stealing, since it is someone else's property. I suggest that she be burned at the stake."

"Trial by jury, then," suggested Joseph. "I will be counsel for the defense. Alfred can be the prosecuting attorney. We need a judge."

"I accept the judgeship," said the magician. "And I suggest that the trial be held tomorrow morning."

Everyone agreed.

"Remember," said Joseph, "that proof is the essential thing; and everyone must tell the truth."

——

After much difficulty I got permission to visit Florence who was in solitary confinement. She lay on her bed looking very pale but smiling happily.

"I came to see how you are," I said.

"It was a boy," she sighed joyfully.

"That's wonderful, and what will you call him?" I asked eagerly.

"Gerard, of course," she answered.

"Can I see him?" I asked.

"You can't have him," she whimpered. "No one can take him away."

"But I . . ." And then, in despair at the misunderstanding, I covered my eyes with my fingers. When I removed my hands with a start, I realized that there was no baby. Not knowing what I had come for, I ran down the corridor into the arms of Sir Phalatrope.

"Florence thinks she has a baby," I said. I broke away and ran into my room to weep.

I wanted it to be true. I wanted Florence to marry Gerard and have a baby. There is nothing to believe any more. I do not want a husband. Joseph is a maniac. He thinks he is a doctor. My husband is a doctor. Sir Phalatrope must not be a doctor. If he was a doctor he could have delivered Florence's child, but since there is no child there is still the possibility that he is a magician and not a doctor. Alfred Blatt detests me because I was not a good teacher. He also thinks I stole things which I never did. He thinks I am stealing Hannah's poems. I wrote them but I gave them to her. I want them back. I do not want a ring. I want a baby but I do not want my husband's baby. He had a vasectomy. I think he did it to himself. I am very upset. I do not know anything. I do not know whether to entertain my clients tonight. I don't have to wear the costume any more. I can wear what I please. But if I don't do that what will I do? There is nothing to do any more. I have no husband and I have no mother. If there is no magician to help me I cannot live any longer. Joseph thinks I am deceived by him. I am not deceived by anything now. But I want to be deceived. What happens now? And when they put me on trial for stealing the poetry I may be found guilty and burned at the stake. I don't care if I am burned at the stake. It is better than being with people.

Because of the chaos that threatened me I stayed in my small room. I did not know the time nor had I decided upon my evening's activity.

"I have discovered something beyond the erotic manual," I had told Florence. I was still uncertain what it was. I will no longer appease my husband Joseph by performing downstairs, I decided.

I have destroyed the erotic manual. I am only myself. I tremble when I write it. Is this my discovery—a bare, formless thing with no purpose or connection to anyone? I am only myself. Nothing is more terrifying. Some irrevocable amputation has been achieved.

I closed my notebook and tried to imagine the clients applauding my performance. "I must entertain my customers," I whispered to myself. "Where is the book of rules, the examinations and penalties?" I said in a louder tone, clenching the blanket with my sweating palm.

There was a hesitant knock at the door. I did not answer.

"It is Joseph, your defense attorney."

"I am only myself," I said as I opened the door. "Who are you?"

"I am the counsel appointed for your defense," he said.

I laughed, recognizing the husky laugh of Madelaine. Joseph withdrew, but I knew how to deal with false identities.

"Oh yes," I said, smiling. "I've been expecting you, since my trial begins tomorrow."

"May I take off my hat and show you some of the briefs I have carefully prepared for your defense?" he asked.

I nodded.

"I've met with District Attorney Blatt, and he has given me a long list of your felonies and misdemeanors."

"A list," I exclaimed. "I thought it was a simple question of whether or not I had stolen my own poetry from Hannah."

"Well, that is the main purpose of tomorrow's trial, but you are also charged with grand larceny—an enormous quantity of stolen marmalade, erasers, rubber bands, and toilet paper. Let me see, oh yes: negligence in the classroom, destruction of school property, prostitution, and manslaughter."

Joseph sat down on the bed, exhausted. "You must have faith in me," he said.

"I've killed no one, except a gynecologist," I protested, weeping, "and surely that's not a crime." But I remembered something else—a murder in a circular tower. "Rope and a steel bar," I said.

"Don't worry about it," said Joseph. "You need not prove your innocence. In our state, under our constitution, it is up to those who prosecute to prove your guilt . . . beyond a reasonable doubt," he added, looking more like a gynecologist each second.

"What state are you talking about?"

"It's of no importance," answered Joseph, pushing me on to the examining table and letting his briefs drop to the floor.

"Trust me," he said as he turned on the harsh metallic light.

Later he put on his hat, collected his briefs, shook my hand, and left.

HANNAH VS. ELAINE

THE TRIAL FOR POETRY

No one was allowed to go below the green corridor on the evening before the trial.

"The courtroom is being prepared," announced Sir Phalatrope.

It was a peaceful evening. Mrs. Gilligan played dominoes with Gerard. And Florence, to my delight, was up and about, chatting with my mother about her recent miscarriage.

"I had one too, thank heavens," I heard my mother say.

Alfred Blatt sat in a corner filling card after card with observations and accusations. Occasionally he muttered, "Nobody's daughter, the duck will be slaughtered," or "Bone for bone, eye for eye, creator of sorrow I'll drown her tomorrow."

Joseph, hard at work, said nothing, but gave me what he thought were reassuring glances.

The magician wandered from room to room.

"Are you nervous about the trial?" he asked me with some concern. I smiled. He studied me very carefully. "You are coming closer to yourself. The trial may test some of your new insights."

"I hate that word," I said.

He laughed. "Try not to be so perfectionistic. Then you will be able to fight your real prosecutor."

Dr. Phalatrope is an ordinary man. He does not know what he is doing, but sometimes he succeeds by accident. Joseph is not my husband. I hate my husband. Joseph is no one. I will leave this house by my own means only if I do not allow the others to convince me of anything false. I was a terrible kindergarten teacher. I won't teach any more. Alfred Blatt was not the principal of P.S. X. I knew that all the time, but he is like him. Gerard is an aide who can't find employment elsewhere. He has nothing to do with Florence. I am afraid the trial will confuse everyone and make me stay here forever. I will not give my poems away any more. I will write my own poem now.

A POEM BY ELAINE

Time has forged broken chains
    World or not
Half-entwined
    I struggle.

No night or day
To my hands.
        Forever?

Madelaine's fled
Magician's dead
    (Birth and death)
    (All at once.)

Broken rings bind my throat
    (tarnished gold.)
Pierce my tongue
    I struggle.

No night or day
World or not
Magician's fled
Rubber hands dead
Forever?

(Birth and death)
(All at once.)
I vanish.

I was about to fall asleep when Joseph opened my door, presenting me with two pink carnations, whitish brown, withered at the edges and dark purple in the centers.

"You are my flower," he said, and ran blushing from the room.

I laughed so loudly that Gerard knocked to see that everything was all right. He gave me another Seconal. I fell asleep with the lamp on, staring at the dying flowers.

The next morning I scribbled a few things and crossed out most of them.

Beyond the erotic manual is a flower. I love Joseph. Today is the trial of dead flowers, the trial of light, the dead who live. Today is the trial of lies—all words are lies.

I was dragged down the spiraling staircase to the courtroom below and hidden in a small chamber behind heavy drapes. Someone whose head was covered like a hangman handcuffed me. My defense attorney told me that it was just a formality. He and Alfred Blatt paced the room, avoiding each other's eyes but watching the huge clock above.

I peered out of a hole in the thick black curtain that separated us from the rest of the courtroom, and watched the jury filing in from another antechamber. I recognized them at once; the men in pin-striped suits, their moustaches growing with bristling certainty from hot, dilated pores. A few women were familiar in fuchsia net with breasts raised above tight whalebone girdles.

The courtroom was hot and I noticed the women catching the wax breasts that had begun to melt and molding them into more compact shapes. One juror's moustache slipped down and embedded itself in his chin.

"Some air conditioning, please," he asked the court stenographer, who took down the question verbatim and then turned a knob behind the jury box. It was a blast so cold that everything froze as it was; half-formed breasts still being sculpted congealed, and heads not yet smoothed from the indentation of tight derby hats retained harsh lines.

"Isn't that going too far?" asked a juror whose mouth cracked as he spoke.

After recording this remark, the stenographer readjusted the temperature. They sighed in unison—twelve jurors and a spare.

"They have been most carefully chosen and questioned," my defense attorney told me. "And they are all well versed in the constitution and the penal code," he reassured.

I was then led to a table in the main room by the masked man. Joseph sat next to me, our backs to the spectators who were rapidly filling the courtroom. Alfred Blatt sat at a table adjacent to the jury box. He stretched his neck in order to leer at the women inside. He waved to one and winked. She winked back, but that eye stuck to the lower lid and throughout the trial it remained closed. Joseph frowned at this sign of collusion between the D.A. and the female jurors. But he whispered comforting things into my ear. None of it made any sense.

A hush filled the courtroom as Sir Phalatrope in a velvet jeweled robe and a crown on his head climbed the ladder to the judge's throne. I wanted to applaud this spectacle, but the handcuffs would not permit it.

"Will the court rise," came from a hidden tape recorder. Everyone obeyed. "Be seated."

"Henceforth," said the judge, "the jury shall not be seated until after I present myself."

The jurors hung their heads and blushed with shame, causing some disturbance of their features.

"Today we begin the trial of the state against Elaine."

"What state?" I asked Joseph. But he said it was insignificant.

"The prosecution may proceed," said Judge Phalatrope, looking down at Alfred Blatt. Alfred rose promptly.

"I would like to call the plaintiff, Hannah, to the stand."

A roar went up in the courtroom and Judge Phalatrope pounded his gavel to restore order.

"Do you swear the testimony you are about to give is the whole truth and nothing but the truth?" asked the tape.

"I do," said Hannah, taking the stand.

"Your name?"

"Hannah."

"It takes a lover to find another. Without a mother, we'll slaughter the daughter," said Alfred Blatt.

"Objection," shouted Joseph.

"Objection sustained," said the Judge. "I will ask the prosecuting attorney to please attempt to follow court procedure."

"Will you please tell the court about the transaction that occurred between you and the duck the ninth day of the eighth month, when the moon was eclipsed," continued D.A. Blatt.

"She came up to my tower where I was sleeping. She woke me up and gave me a book of poems. You are a poet now, she said. I took the poems and signed my name to them."

"You are then the author of these poems?"

"Objection," shouted Joseph.

"Objection sustained. That is a conclusion to be reached or rejected by the jury. The jury is counseled to disregard the implication of the last question of D.A. Blatt," said the judge.

The jurors smiled and clapped their hands.

"Did the defendant give you any more poetry after the event on the night of the lunar eclipse?" asked Alfred.

"Yes. Each night she slipped one on my lap during dinner. I signed it, put it inside my brassiere, and then read it," said Hannah.

"Your witness," said Alfred. He sat down to file his finger nails.

Joseph got up to cross-examine Hannah. When he stood before her, Hannah turned her head so it faced the ante-chambers behind the judge.

"Will the plaintiff please face the defense attorney," said Judge Phalatrope in a gentle voice.

Hannah giggled, faced Joseph, and then stuck her tongue out. Joseph proceeded nevertheless.

"Have you ever written poetry prior to the receipt of these poems from the defendant?"

"Objection," shouted Alfred Blatt, stamping his foot and dropping his nail file. "The question is misleading and irrelevant to establishing authorship of these poems. And may I remind the defense that theft, not authorship, is the main issue."

"Objection sustained," said the judge after some thought.

"Your Honor, I think the question of authorship very pertinent," said Joseph.

"You, Hannah, said in your testimony that the defendant gave you a book of her poems and said, you are a poet now. Is that correct?"

Hannah began to cry.

"Please answer," urged the judge, bending over and handing her a handkerchief engraved with gold horses.

"Objection," shouted D.A. Blatt in a fury. "The plaintiff said she was given a book of poems by the defendant. She did not say the poems were written by the defendant." ·

Judge Phalatrope asked the court stenographer to read back Hannah's testimony.

"You are correct. Objection sustained," he said.

"Anything written in green ink by a thieving duck is bound to stink," Alfred muttered under his breath. (The jurors howled with laughter.)

"I have an exhibit if it will please the court to label it," said Joseph.

"Objection," cried Alfred. "It is not time for the defense's exhibits."

Judge Phalatrope stroked his beard. "I declare an exception. Objection overruled."

"Exhibit HF2," said one of the court clerks.

"Do you recognize these, Hannah?" asked Joseph.

"The poems. I mean, my poems."

"Are all of them your poems? Examine them carefully."

Hannah leafed through the carbons and hesitated.

Alfred looked at her and chanted, "She'll tremble and quake when burned at the stake. We'll roast the duck who stole the poems."

"Order, please," commanded Judge Phalatrope. "Remember, Hannah, you are under oath and you must not perjure yourself."

"They're all mine. I recognize them," said Hannah, trembling. Then she burst into violent sobbing. "No, no, I don't recognize all of them. I never wrote them . . . but I won't give them back." She swooned and Sir Phalatrope recessed the court for ten minutes.

Alfred Blatt was under his table, biting his newly painted nails and crying furiously. Hannah was removed to a back room to be revivified.

I watched the jury filing out; a woman lingered. She had forgotten one of her legs, which was stuck to the juror's bench. She wept, her tears melting the leg. Blushing with shame, she took it with her to the Ladies' Room.

Judge Phalatrope disappeared.

The court reconvened in twenty minutes. Everyone was refreshed and alert. The lady juror was smoothing her leg into its proper socket. Pleased with its shape, she lifted her skirts.

Alfred Blatt was calmly watching Hannah, who was composed if a little tipsy in the witness chair. And Judge Phalatrope was majestically sipping water on his throne.

"May I continue the cross-examination, Your Honor?" asked Joseph.

"Proceed," said the judge.

"Hannah, will you please read any of the poems that you do not recognize."

Alfred frowned, and Hannah stood up as she was accustomed to when she read. Judge Phalatrope motioned to her to be seated.

> I am Elaine
> I think I am
> A she-ape turned woman
> Sheep or dam
> Who traveled far
> To reach this realm
> To rescue Florence
> From her mother-wolf not lamb
> And from her husband
> But a sham
> A gynecologist
> By all despised named Joseph
> Who with lecherous eyes
> Creates a world of pinching corsets
> Mashed breasts and burning sphincters
> Plunged into with a feather
> Which feels like a cylinder of leather
> Who left my bed when all was calm
> To do a thousand women harm
> To make messy hysterectomies

> and X ray Fallopian Tubes needlessly
> To see them writhe in bed with shame
> And watch rehearsals for his manual's game.
> But I am I think Elaine
> Here I am and here I came
> To the house of Madelaine.

The jury applauded politely, with downcast eyes, and Florence wept hidden among the spectators.

"That is all," said Joseph.

"The witness may step down," ordered the Judge.

Hannah stumbled into Alfred's arms. He turned away.

"It takes a lover to know a liar," he said, winking at the female juror, who was etching a flower pattern in her leg.

Alfred displayed his fury at Hannah for admitting that she did not recognize some of her poetry, by stealing my lunch. Sir Phalatrope watched to see my reaction. I ignored Alfred. More disturbing to me was my husband who was sitting next to me. He had evidently come from examining a female patient. He offered me half of his lunch with a simplicity that was meant to disarm me.

"Keep your food. I remember everything now," I said, not at all interested in the insinuations Alfred was making about my theft.

"Do you remember the wedding night?" asked Dr. Phalatrope, moving closer. I laughed and went into my room to rest and write before the trial resumed.

Dr. Phalatrope did a stupid thing by pretending to agree that Joseph is my husband. I am well aware that Joseph is some schizophrenic who doesn't know who he is and that my husband does not have a beard or blue eyes. Sometimes I am confused, but I am not as crazy as Dr. Phalatrope thinks. I am angry and disgusted at him for not realizing how much I know. Even while I am believing something I can tell if it is false. He has no right to manipulate people like this.

I closed my notebook and lay down with a headache.

Dr. Phalatrope knocked.

"You can no longer read what I write," I told him.

He looked confused.

"Why do you allow people to think things that are lies. Why do you encourage them?" I scream at him.

"They come to see the truth all alone when they are ready," he said.

"My husband, not Joseph, was very gentle on our wedding night. He said, however, that I should have emptied my stools and that he would have liked my vagina to be a little longer. He examined me thoroughly, holding me open with the speculum. He said he loved me very much and that we would share everything. I think he meant it."

"But he was too sick to treat anyone with real consideration," said Dr. Phalatrope as he left for his judicial chambers.

———

One of the jurors was constipated. Time passed slowly as we waited. He finally appeared, looking apologetic, and the trial proceeded.

Gerard was called by my defense attorney. His wife, Florence, sat in the first row during his testimony.

"Will it please you to tell the court what you observed on the evening of the day, seven months subsequent to the night of the lunar eclipse?" asked Joseph.

"I saw the defendant holding a poem in her lap. The plaintiff reached for it as she had done on other occasions. The defendant hesitated but did not give up the poem."

"And who read the poem on that occasion?"

"The defendant did."

"Did you see the defendant steal any poems from the plaintiff on that evening?"

"No, I did not."

"You may step down," said Joseph.

Florence clapped enthusiastically. But Gerard looked into space.

"Gerard," called Florence, waving her hand.

The jurors laughed, with the exception of the one who had been constipated. Judge Phalatrope pounded his gravel.

"Husbands are very cruel," I said, and the judge motioned to me to be silent.

D.A. Blatt stepped up to cross-examine Gerard.

"Haven't you had sexual relations with the defendant?" he asked.

"Objection," called Joseph, as Florence fainted and was carried from the courtroom.

"Objection sustained."

"Well, I have," said Alfred, with a vindictive grimace.

"Liar," I shouted, standing up.

"The jury is counseled to disregard the question and the statement of the D.A.," said Judge Phalatrope.

"Why should we?" asked the juror with the flowered leg.

"Because it is hearsay," said the judge.

"If she's a whore, then we have a right to know," persisted the juror.

"Order. This case will rest until obedient jurors can be found," said Judge Phalatrope. After the jury filed into the anteroom, he stepped down and removed his crown and robes.

———

The case rested for several weeks. I learned from Joseph that new jurors were being sought, and that Hannah, recognizing that the weight of evidence rested in my favor, had dropped the complaint. In fact she had returned all my poems with her signature crossed out.

"But you are being charged with manslaughter," said Joseph, patting my hand.

"He deserved to die," I said, thinking of my husband, whom I had murdered many times in fantasy.

"You are not going to confess!" Joseph said in alarm.

"Whatever I please," I answered, and laughed as he left. Having nothing better to do I wrote a poem about the murder.

> The man I murdered is not dead.
> I see his hands and villainous head
> Who trained me in erotic perfection
> With whip in hand for quick correction
> The man I killed walks with a rope
> His name is Doctor Phalatrope.
> In dreams I see him with his tools
> His lab, his table, female ghouls
> Bound and gagged with metal rings
> He's armed with curettes, dilators, gouges, springs.
> I retch but speechless play his game.
> Waking I do not know my name. I think
> That it is Madelaine.

"Lie on this table," said my husband. "No, stupid, keep your heels on so you can put them through the stirrups."

He abducted my legs.

"Must I?" I asked timidly, as the high voltage lamp was turned on at the foot of the table.

He inserted the cervical tenaculum and withdrew it.

"Must I?"

There was no answer as he slipped on his thin rubber gloves, covered them with lubricating jelly, and mounted. Nor could I speak. Something—a huge gold ring—was inserted in my mouth. I lay inert hearing the clanking noise of the various specula as he exchanged one for another. Finally, I was paralyzed by his intensity and by the pleasure which totally excluded me.

"Very good. No cysts or nodules to speak of," he said as he removed the gloves and closed the metallic clasp at the top of his fly. I was allowed to get off the table.

———

Dinners were silent. I carefully prepared what he liked, making certain to sterilize all plates and utensils in his presence. He demanded that I wash my hands with disinfectant soap. Although it burned my skin, I felt no justification in complaining.

During dinner he read recent publications from conferences on obstetrics and gynecology. I sat nibbling in tense silence, hoping he would not question me. Often when he appeared thoroughly engrossed in his papers the cross-examination would begin.

"Describe the function of Bartholin's glands."

Seeing my confusion he laughed, moustache bristling from dilated pores.

"The ducts from yours are a bit congested and no doubt I'll have to replace them with plastic ducts very soon."

I trembled and stopped eating.

"Eat," he commanded. I forced the food into my mouth.

"Where did you hide your Papanicolaou report?" he would ask accusingly.

To satisfy his requirement, his love and concern, I had to have a thorough pelvic examination and a Pap smear taken each month by the top specialist in uterine malignancies.

"I didn't get the report yet."

"Liar, thief," he accused, stamping his feet. Then he engrossed himself in his reading for the rest of the meal.

———

Eventually the ducts became engorged, as he had predicted, and plastic ones were inserted, quite expertly, during an operation he performed on the examining table in our bedroom.

"False duct," he called me affectionately after that. Later it changed to "duck."

"How are your plastic tubes, duck?" he would ask from beneath his moustache.

"Fine," I answered.

"I should say so. Secretory function unimpaired."

I didn't tell him that in one of the books I was forced to read there was some question as to whether Bartholin's glands had any secretory function at all.

—

Dr. Phalatrope did not think I was ready to stand trial again. He visited me every day.

"Get away from my ovaries," I would shout, and obligingly he moved to a far corner of my room.

"I am not your wife any longer and you cannot silence me."

Dr. Phalatrope said nothing. He left when I asked him to and seemed sorry for what he had done to me.

BETWEEN TRIALS

A feeling of suspension as well as disorganization pervaded the house. Gerard was restless and no longer played dominoes with Mrs. Gilligan. When engaged in a game of bridge or checkers with one of the others, he often glanced at his wrist watch, making sure it corresponded with the large wall clock to the second. He spoke little and kept to himself except for the duties which he was forced to perform, such as distributing colored pills in pleated cups or administering the hypodermic syringe when I needed adrenalin.

Hannah and Alfred had not spoken to each other since the trial, although she gave him longing, furtive glances when he was not looking in her direction. Dr. Phalatrope was displeased; he had been counting upon their relationship to accomplish some end, and made abortive attempts at effecting a reconciliation between them. It was of no avail. Alfred was totally engrossed in his growing obsession—my destruction. And he no longer considered Hannah an ally since she had forfeited my poetry. Late into the night he scribbled his plans on lined cards—elegantly, incisively, in green ink. Nor did he allow them to lie scattered on the floor in disarray; he kept them under lock and key in a gray metallic box that he had stolen from Joseph.

Florence was receiving mysterious treatments in the isolation room so I never saw her. Gerard grudgingly brought her meals into the room on a plastic tray. Once I saw Gerard and Dr. Phalatrope carrying a box with peculiar wires extending from its seams. It was too small to be a coffin so I didn't worry about it.

My mother seemed to think this box or toy had humorous possibilities and convulsed into hysterical laughter whenever she caught a glimpse of it. I laughed too, in order to ingratiate myself with her. As ever she toyed with the pansies, stubbornly refusing to acknowledge my existence. I kept the water fresh for her and picked up the dead pansies that surrounded her chair.

Even Joseph remained alone. Perhaps he was preparing my new defense. I didn't believe it or trust him.

Meals were silent; the silence broken occasionally by Mrs. Gilligan, who thought she heard the voice of one of her dead relatives and urged us to listen. Sometimes she had a warning for someone that she had chanced upon in her crystal ball or worked out carefully on an astrological chart.

"Murder, theft, sin, and violence," she often chanted, staring at me. I shuddered as one thousand visions passed through my mind but I continued eating.

The table was set, as usual, for nine. Nine seldom appeared. The setting was careless; the beige cloth had dark stains like stale blood, and the forks were bent and half-washed. Missing napkins, moldy bread, empty grapefruit skins, burned fowl, brown lettuce were all ignored. It didn't matter; we ate swiftly and then vanished into various rooms, always alone.

But I am not certain. Perhaps it was my own vision that dispersed each into an indivisible atom of anger. Maybe they danced, laughed, and embraced each other, apart from my hideous vision. I doubt it; I never heard music, and no sound came from below—no thunderous applause, songs, twirling plumage, screeching masks. The trial had expelled all the gaiety of my transformation. I missed it.

One day, in desperation, I searched my closet for costumes. No, there were only a few dresses and a blue robe that my husband had given me when we were engaged. I tore it to bits.

Silence, emptiness, and time moving more slowly each day. Endless space broken by a distant wail from Florence, a wheeze, a sudden vision revealed by Mrs. Gilligan or an occasional outburst of angry cursing and sobbing from Alfred Blatt. They were always angry, throwing crayons at each other, whirling paper planes, tearing up and down the room like caged lions. I stood by helplessly, my marriage band burning my finger as a broken crayon hit me on the forehead.

"Control your class," said Mr. Blatt, the principal. "I can bring no important visitors into this room." He glanced at the waste basket that had been overturned and at the paint smeared over floor and tables. "We used to have an orderly school." Looking as if he wanted to murder me, he closed the door.

At lunch time I picked up the crayons from the floor, replacing them in each child's orange juice can. It was necessary that they all be in order. Then I straightened the room and wiped the paint from the floor with an old sponge.

"I'm sorry I won't have time to go out for lunch today," I would say to the kindergarten teacher next door who looked at me with pity and disdain.

Carefully I traced dark lipstick over my mouth. My eyes were undefined; I felt them twitching in a characteristic spasm as I brushed chalk dust from my blue linen dress with its high ruffled collar.

"You'll never make a teacher," said my husband, scraping the fetus from my womb and putting two penicillin injections into my buttocks. A few days later, he performed a vasectomy upon himself.

"We must have no more of this nonsense. I'm a busy man."

I am in the house of silence. There is endless space without movement backward or forward. What has happened to time? The clock on the wall does not move any longer. No one ever laughs or cries. I believe that the magician has died but I am afraid to find out because then I will be left alone. Will he bequeath his white horse to me? I know there is no horse. In ten days I stand trial for manslaughter. Is it another one of the magician's tricks? I cannot remember who I murdered. Perhaps I will find out from one of the witnesses. But they are all ... no no even that does not matter. The evenings are dull anguish; silence, breaking of pens stuck too hard into cards which proclaim my guilt, rustling of pages, falling of tiles and dominoes raining on silver-smooth tables, scurrying of mice imprisoned in walls, moans from distant corners, clicking of metallic lamps, smothering gray blankets, and heavy cold golden rings around my throat.

"Beyond the erotic manuals of my husband is my death," I wrote on a piece of paper which I handed to Dr. Phalatrope. (I no longer spoke.)

"Why don't you speak?" he asked, looking defeated.

"Speech leads to error, miscalculation, accusation, violence, and extinction," I wrote.

"You mean you will no longer take the risk involved in order to exist."

Angrily I pointed to the word "extinction."

"I understand how quickly your efforts at affirmation led to extinction," said Dr. Phalatrope thoughtfully.

"No one can react to a mummy," exploded my husband, banging his elbows on the table. "Say something."

He had just received an honorary award for his invention of the plastic duct.

"You are lucky," he said. "Another gynecologist would have removed the non-functioning duct and the gland as well."

"Thank you," I said, feeling something tightening my larynx.

"Laryngismus," laughed my husband.

———

The principal was sending an "experienced" teacher to help me with my sub-standard classroom organization.

"Thank you," I blurted out, before my rage could strangle me.

"Don't cry like an infant, little duck," said my husband with a demonic leer. "When I finish my research I will put fresh tissue on the examining table. Meanwhile you can put on your yellow feathered gown and polish the stirrups. Oh, yes," he said, rubbing his hands together in anticipation, "don't forget to sterilize the dilator, speculum, and aspiration bulb."

"Your room must be divided into areas," said the great teacher. At her entrance the children had become docile and obedient. They crayoned neat pictures of carrot-nosed snowmen which she stapled efficiently in a row across the back of the room.

"Where is your calendar?" I shook my head with shame as she unrolled one from her purse—click, click. Five apples take away three. Four grapefruits take away seven.

"Your wrist watch?" She stared reprovingly at my naked wrists.

Some of the children wept quietly, while others, glad to relinquish their freedom, happily pasted circles of red and blue as she commanded.

"Your room must be divided into areas," said the greatings. "The room looks neat and orderly and the children are busily at work," he sighed, happily pinching her corseted buttocks.

"Of course, it is your class and you must teach in your own way," said the master teacher. "I wouldn't dream of imposing my own methods; I'm just here to help."

"Just to make sure there is no cellular malignancy," said my husband, withdrawing the aspiration bulb with satisfaction. "It is all for your own good," he said, swabbing my bleeding cervix with a cotton-tipped applicator dipped in saline solution. No sound from my lips, whirling instruments shining into my eyes as I fainted at the scream accompanying his ejaculation.

"You should be very happy," he said at breakfast. "The squamous epithelium is very rich in glycogen. I'll have your yellow gown cleaned," he said, putting it into his briefcase and kissing me good-bye.

Dr. Phalatrope wants to help me. What does that mean? Didn't my husband help me by further experiments when the master teacher took away everything. But he scraped the fetus from me without my consent and took away my voice. I don't want a voice. What will Dr. Phalatrope scrape away? I am more afraid now than ever.

In the starless gray of the evening, an art historian came to my door ready to deliver a lecture. His arms were bursting with projectors, broken pointers, black slide boxes, and crushed folders of catalogued notes. He smiled, his breath smelling of an antiseptic solution.

"I am ready to begin," he said, tapping me on my head with the rubber tip of the pointer.

"Go away. I refuse to be lectured to. I will not take notes. I will enter the painting if I please."

He was shocked, and trembled at the vulgarity of that idea.

"Preserve the plane, preserve the plane," he muttered angrily.

"Disappear. You are part of my past," I screamed, forcing him to join hands with my husband and the "master teacher."

They surrounded me in a circle. I sang in spite of their jeering laughter. Straining against their derisive shouts, I sang the noisy children to sleep. The rubber gloves melted into the floorboards, the "master teacher's" corset blew up into fragments and disappeared. Joseph, the art historian, lingered, dropping his briefs. I threw them at him and slammed the door.

> Sleep children sleep
> The sun has gone away
> Butterflies are
> Embalmed in ice
> Silent moths still play.

Weep children weep
The stars that once did glow
Have fallen into a pool of blood
Flowers will not grow.

Sleep babies sleep
Though spring has gone away
Those hands that bound
Your hands and tongues
Have faded into gray.

Sleep children sleep
The sun has gone away
Colors are embalmed in ice
But tired sparrows play.

They slept soundly and smiled in their dreams.

—

When everything was quiet, Dr. Phalatrope came inside.

"I have sent them away," I whispered, glancing around to make sure.

"You mean the people who have kept you silent?"

"All the dead phantoms," I answered.

"Is it really necessary to dismiss everyone before you can speak?" he asked.

"I know they, my silencers, are only my phantoms," I said calmly.

"But they are real to you nevertheless."

"What do you want of me, Dr. Phalatrope? Isn't it enough that I realize what they are? Must I believe it?"

"It could be easier for you if you believed it, but I don't expect that much yet."

"Maybe I will never really believe that they have not silenced me, Dr. Phalatrope."

"I hope you will," he said.

TRIAL FOR MANSLAUGHTER

THE STATE VS. ELAINE

The jury had been selected for my new trial; I eyed them suspiciously, as before, from behind the moth-eaten velvet curtain. They were constructed rigidly, and looked anxious to obey the rules of the court. Legs, arms, and heads seemed securely fastened, and the men's moustaches were waxed and turned up sharply in tiny pin points.

Judge Phalatrope, wearing purple robes and a heavy crown, surveyed the courtroom to see that all was as it should be. He motioned to the bailiff, who oiled the mechanical hearts, brains, and other apparatus of the jurors. Then he polished their appendages.

"I wish to be sworn in," demanded Alfred Blatt.

"Objection," shouted Joseph. "The District Attorney cannot take the stand."

Judge Phalatrope pulled at his white beard. "I don't see why not," he said thoughtfully. "Proceed."

"Two hundred and ninety-one days ago I was murdered in a tower," testified D.A. Blatt after being sworn in. "The murderer is in this courtroom," he said, pointing to me. "In my opinion I should be permitted to testify on my own behalf, in view of her heinous crime. After all, I've given her several pedicures and restyled her hair. I regret it now . . . I regret it bitterly," he sobbed.

"Can you produce the murder weapon?" asked the judge.

The jury stared with frozen pupils as Alfred Blatt drew from beneath his immaculate collar and tie a bristly rope stained with blood.

"Without provocation of any sort, she assaulted me with this. I meant to let the matter go, but her conduct in all things is so vile that I cannot let it rest." A profusion of tears and sobs came from him. The jurors pulled out freshly ironed handkerchiefs and joined in the tempest. (The bailiff poured additional oil into their sockets when they had finished.)

Alfred stepped down and took his seat as State Prosecutor.

"Your Honor, I would like to cross-examine this witness," said Joseph, my counselor.

"How can you cross-examine a dead man?" asked Alfred. "You may weep for him. He was a noble fellow, indeed, but cross-examination is out of the question." (All the jurors and witnesses had begun to weep afresh.)

"Your Honor," said Joseph, "something is wrong with this proceeding and I ask that you consult the penal code."

"The proceedings will proceed as they must. I will only intervene on matters of great importance," answered the judge.

"District Attorney Blatt, you may call your eyewitness."

Hannah, looking tired from weeping, was sworn in.

"Are you Hannah?" asked D.A. Blatt, with some hostility.

"Yes, and a poet by grace of the defendant for a time until she stole the poetry that she gave me. I am no longer a poet and have generously dropped those charges against the fiend."

"Why did you drop those charges?" shouted the D.A., glaring at her.

"Irrelevant," said Joseph.

"A matter of opinion," argued Alfred with spite.

"Objection overruled," declared Judge Phalatrope.

"In my grief over the loss of my beloved Alfred Blatt, I no longer considered the theft of any importance."

"How noble and unselfish," the spectators whispered to each other.

"Did you see your beloved Alfred Blatt murdered?" asked Alfred, his tone softening.

"Yes," answered Hannah.

"Please tell the court what you saw on that terrible night two hundred and ninety-one days ago."

"I was fast asleep when the murder was committed," stated Hannah.

A roar of surprised exclamations and confusion went up in the courtroom. The judge called them back to attention. Some squeaks were heard as the jurors struggled into silence.

Alfred Blatt, livid with rage, continued. "An eyewitness cannot be asleep. Proceed with the testimony as rehearsed."

"Objection," said Joseph, chewing his pencil in exasperation. But the judge was snoring heavily.

"I was asleep, but I had one eye open all the time," amended Hannah, regaining her composure. "She (she pointed her finger at me) crept into the secret chamber where Alfred and I were spending our honeymoon; she put the rope around his neck, knotted it, and pulled until he turned blue. Then she laughed and carried the body out of the room."

Alfred smiled and bowed to Hannah. "That is all," he said.

Joseph stepped up to cross-examine her.

"Was the chamber dark on the night of the murder?"

"Pitch black," she answered.

"And yet you testified that you saw the defendant's face, with one eye open?"

"I can see in the dark and even with both eyes closed," asserted Hannah.

"Then why did you do nothing to stop the murder of your bridegroom, Alfred Blatt?"

"We'd had a strenuous night and I just couldn't be bothered to wake myself up and go chasing a murderer."

"Is Alfred Blatt a strong man, in your opinion?"

"Even a bit rough at times," she said, laughing.

"And the defendant?" asked Joseph.

"A scarecrow, a skinny evil bird."

"One last question—is the deceased in this courtroom?"

"Bless his soul in heaven," said Hannah, pointing to the table where the D.A. had been seated. It was empty. Alfred Blatt was nowhere in the courtroom.

"No," said Hannah, with some alarm.

"That is all."

Judge Phalatrope awoke and rubbed his eyes. "You may step down, Hannah," he said. Then he recessed the court for ten minutes.

Alfred Blatt sat alone in the green corridor, eating a piece of toast and marmalade. "Oh dear, I've smeared my nail lacquer," he muttered to himself.

"I have murdered my husband, and I wish to confess," I said, tugging at Sir Phalatrope's robes as he passed.

"A harmless misdemeanor," he whispered, absorbed in his own thoughts.

"I will not testify," my mother was telling Joseph. "I gave her everything. If she's a whore and a husband slayer, that's no concern of mine."

"Mother," I pleaded, bending over her still figure. Then I placed my fingers over my eyes to blot out her indifference. When I opened my eyes, I was astonished. There sat a grotesque and pitiful form, no one's mother.

"Joseph, she's not my mother. Don't you understand?" I began to cry and rushed into my room.

Dr. Phalatrope came to see me. "She's incurable," he said. "It is true that she does not want to see you as you are. Try to stop summoning her. I think it will help you."

"Who will defend me?" I asked.

"Joseph will try, in his own way. I will make an attempt. You

can always find someone. But for the most part you must defend
yourself."

"I cannot," I said. His words made me feel very lonely. But
Joseph came to summon me back to the courtroom, where I was
to take the stand.

———

"Killer, the murderer, the strangler, whore, and slayer." Shouts
were heard in the courtroom, flashbulbs blinded me, boos and
hisses resounded as I approached the stand.

"Do you swear that the testimony you are about to give is the
whole truth and nothing but the truth . . ." blabbed the hidden
tape recorder.

I hesitated. "The whole truth and nothing but the truth. I
must think it over for a moment," I said, overwhelmed by the
import of the phrase. The stenographer stretched his fingers and
the entire court laughed and booed. Joseph frowned silently. "Is
it possible to exact the whole truth?" I asked myself aloud.

"Don't be so perfectionistic," whispered the judge while the
jury stamped electric stumps in impatient unison. (There had
not been time to complete the feet.) Yielding to the pressures
about me, I allowed myself to be sworn in. "Truth is such a
changeable commodity," I whispered dubiously to Judge Phalatrope, who ignored me.

Seated, scanning the courtroom for familiar faces—Gerard,
Florence, my mother—I saw the huge figure of Madelaine;
she appeared on a rostrum at the back of the courtroom, grinning and applauding loudly. Tiny, powerful lights gleamed from
the intricately jeweled snake bracelet. "Madelaine," I screamed.
But at the sound of her name, she disappeared. I touched my
bracelet; its ruby-eyed snake threw his own evil glint into my
eyes.

"Did you or did you not murder Alfred Blatt?" asked Joseph
nervously.

"I did not, but I know I murdered someone," I said.

"Where were you on that night approximately five thousand seven hundred and eighty-four hours ago?"

"I was entertaining my clients in the Victorian . . ."

"That's sufficient," said Joseph, preventing me from telling the whole truth.

"Whore," shouted the women in the jury box, while the pin-striped men hung their heads, blushing.

"I will ask the jurors to listen in silence," ordered the judge.

The jurors pressed their lips tightly together.

"Did you know the deceased?" asked Joseph.

"He was the principal of P.S. X, where I taught kindergarten."

"Will you describe your relations with Principal Blatt?"

"Objection," said the D.A. "I will not have my reputation fouled and slandered when I am not here to defend myself."

"Rest in peace, rest in peace, rest in peace," chanted the spectators, and Hannah dropped on her knees to pray.

"Objection is overruled," said Judge Phalatrope.

"Principal Blatt objected to my methods. Because I would not keep the children in rows he tried to murder me with a steel drafting ruler."

"The cards must be in rows," mumbled Alfred.

"I have no more questions," said Joseph.

"Well I do, and the sooner I ask them the better," stated D.A. Blatt.

"Proceed," said the judge.

"First I would like to remind you, my duck, that you are under oath. Did you murder Alfred Blatt two hundred and ninety-one evenings ago?"

"No. He was never my husband."

"But you would describe your attitude to the deceased as un-cordial?"

"Yes. He tried to silence me in the classroom."

"Your Honor, will you ask this criminal to answer the questions I ask directly and without comment."

"No," replied the judge. "I will allow freedom of expression in my court. I have made certain amendments to court procedure."

"Then how will the jurors know which are the relevant facts?" demanded the D.A. (The jurors cranked their heads and looked up at the judge.)

"They may choose the facts that appeal to their emotions. Common sense judgments have failed in previous trials. I have counseled the jury to rely upon emotions and prejudice, but to do so silently and with equanimity," answered Judge Phalatrope.

Joseph arose at this pronouncement. "I object to your counseling of the jurors. I will not play."

"I object also. Emotions are dangerous," I said.

"In my experience, reason has failed because it completely upsets and confuses the emotions," argued the judge. "False emotions are substituted for real ones for the sake of justice, and we never arrive at the truth. Now proceed with your cross-examination Mr. Blatt."

"I would like to ask you if you recognize this piece of rope," said D.A. Blatt, picking up exhibit HF2 from the table, which was also covered with dead leaves, the head of a white horse, a crystal ball, crayons, a Graves speculum, and a beaded drawstring purse.

"It looks vaguely familiar. I think the children used it to make sling shots to shoot crayons at one another or at me. Or else my husband used it when performing certain rituals and sacrifices . . . I cannot remember if it is mentioned in the erotic or the physiologic manual . . ."

"The defendant is being deliberately obscure. Strike her testimony from the records."

"It will remain," ordered the judge.

"By the coroner's report, Alfred Blatt was murdered at approximately 1:45 a.m. on the night that you were, by your own admission, entertaining clients."

"Objection," said Joseph.

"Overruled," said the judge.

"What time did you finish you work?"

"At midnight," I said.

"That is all," said Alfred.

"The court will recess for lunch and reconvene in one hour."

—

Dr. Phalatrope came to my room during recess.

"Will this trial never end?" I asked him.

"That is up to you to a greater extent than you realize."

"How is that possible? I am not even certain what I am being tried for."

"That's just the point," he said. "You never even thought of protesting the accusation."

"But I did murder my husband," I said.

"If it makes you feel better to think so," he said, and vanished.

After Sir Phalatrope left, I had a strange experience. I lay on my bed, my hands covering my eyes. And I awoke to emptiness. For a moment I could remember nothing, yet the objects in the room gleamed with brilliance. The two withered carnations that Joseph had given me bent gracefully in a jar of water. And the green metal lamp stood securely on my night table. I saw it as it was—every scratch, its golden stem, and the wire that ran gracefully until it found the socket in the wall. How simple it is, I thought, turning the lamp on and off. But I knew it was only a moment until the huge complexity would return.

My sense of what is real is clear at this moment. I see the bent flowers and the metal lamp. The gray cover is soft and the walls are a yellowish-white. This is how things are. Sometimes they recede or magnify themselves, or glow with a thousand invisible iridescent threads. I can sense the past, at this moment, with its real assaults, victimization, and crime. Perhaps it was not so terrible; I am not certain. But in a moment simple events will become misshapen, unrecognizable in their atrocity, magnified until they are lies. Already the moment is passing. I resent the metallic lamp for not shedding warm amber over everything. Its light is harsh and blinding. I rave that the bed is empty of a warm and faithful lover; its soft gray blanket has changed into something that irritates my skin. And the flowers are detestable for their inconstancy, and because I cannot trust the one who gave them. I will always be on trial because I cannot see by ordinary light. I would like to paint the world differently and call things by new names.

I emerged from my room feeling as though something had changed. But I was not sure what it was. Perhaps the trial will not last forever, I thought with little conviction as I returned to take my seat beside Joseph.

"Joseph," I said, as he looked up in surprise, "thank you for the carnations." Hearing this, Sir Phalatrope's crown fell off his head. The court stenographer scampered after him to replace it.

———

The D.A. called Mrs. Gilligan to the stand.

"Where were you, Mrs. Gilligan, on the night that Alfred Blatt was brutally murdered?"

Her black taffeta skirts swished as she crossed her leg, and I glimpsed the filigreed buckle on her pointed shoe. "I was downstairs watching the show and reading my letters," she said.

"Did you see the defendant leave and go up the escalator to the tower?"

"Yes. I had my crystal ball with me and I saw the entire thing."

"Objection," called Joseph. "The jury should be instructed to disregard the evidence as well as the testimony of such a witness."

"Overruled," said the judge. "The jury must regard the testimony of Mrs. Gilligan in the same way as anyone else's testimony."

"I insist on correct procedure, on method and justice," said Joseph, rising.

"You are my husband," I shouted. The judge laughed. "You

share certain traits with the defendant's husband. Continue with your questioning, Mr. Blatt. And let's have no more unnecessary objections from the defense."

"Please tell the court what you saw in your crystal ball," said Alfred.

"I saw an angry burlesque queen and a lot of dead men."

"Who was that burlesque queen? Is she in the courtroom?"

Mrs. Gilligan pointed her finger at me.

"And did you recognize Alfred Blatt among the dead men?"

"Yes. There were many of them; Alfred Blatt was one, the judge was another, Gerard . . ."

"I am only interested in Alfred Blatt. Did you see the murder weapon in the defendant's hand?"

"Oh I see everything in my crystal ball—future, past . . ."

"I am not interested," stormed the D.A., biting his peach finger nails.

Mrs. Gilligan was insulted. "In that case I refuse to testify. After all, I am in control of your fate and I will recalculate your astrological chart."

"I'm certain that there are some people who are very interested in your testimony," said Judge Phalatrope. "Please accept the court's apology and stay on the stand a little longer."

Mrs. Gilligan considered the matter and remained, but Alfred Blatt claimed that he had no more questions.

Joseph stepped up with some reservation to cross-examine Mrs. Gilligan.

"Have you ever heard the defendant threaten the life of Mr. Blatt?"

"I often suggested to her that in my crystal ball it said that she should murder Alfred."

"And did she listen to you?"

"It's up to the stars—whatever happened was predestined, with my help."

"I heard you tell the court that in your crystal ball you saw a burlesque queen, whom you identified as the defendant, surrounded by a group of dead men; is that so?"

"Not exactly. Now that I think of it, they were not dead; they were lying around and she was standing there dancing, with a rope in her hand. Wait a minute; I think it was I who had the rope in my hand. It was really just a string from the rock candies I had finished. She was doing a dance, rather lewd I might add."

I started to protest.

"Mrs. Gilligan, no offense is meant by this question, but did you murder Alfred?"

"No, but the defendant and I talked about it many times."

"Madelaine," I cried out.

The judge looked alarmed and recessed the court for five minutes.

———

"Madelaine has returned," I whispered to myself, opening my closet and searching behind maroon drapes to make sure she was not hiding there.

"Why have you brought Madelaine back?" I asked Sir Phalatrope as he entered the room.

"Mrs. Madelaine Gilligan has never been away," he said.

"That is not what I mean," I said, tearing the carnations to bits." The other Madelaine is here. You saw her on the stand."

"I saw Mrs. Madelaine Gilligan," he said calmly. "You are the only one who saw Madelaine."

"She's come back," I insisted.

"On the contrary," said the magician. "She is leaving you. You borrowed the rage of Mrs. Gilligan until it became your own. Now it is wearing itself out. Once again you see the destructiveness of Madelaine outside yourself."

"I don't understand you," I sobbed. "I won't go back to the courtroom until you send her away."

"Yes, it's very difficult," said Dr. Phalatrope.

"I won't leave this room."

Without warning, he changed the subject. "Oh, I meant to tell you that Gerard is leaving."

"Oh no! What will Florence do without him? Can she go with him?"

"No, you cannot go with Gerard," he said. "You can survive without your husband. He has made you feel helpless, but you really aren't."

"What about Florence?" I insisted.

"She is improving," he said.

—

After he left, I wondered why he had become so harsh. Then I felt a trembling, panicky feeling because of the departure of my husband.

I ran into the hall. "Gerard," I called. "Gerard." But I could not find him. Defeated, I retreated into my room, indifferent to what was going on below.

—

A change occurred during the following weeks of the trial. I discovered that I could summon Madelaine as well as make her vanish whenever I wanted to. She had no more control over my fate. If I became very angry and counterattacked Alfred Blatt, or insulted my silent mother, Madelaine vanished. I felt her bracelet embedded in my flesh, her drawstring purse in my palm. Then I played dominoes with the carcass of the old Madelaine, and her filigreed buckles, lewd suggestions, cruel laughter, and the visions of slaughter within her crystal ball caused me no alarm. But when I was friendly to Joseph, ignored Alfred's remarks, or displayed affection for my withdrawn mother, Madelaine would appear; then she would command and I would listen in terror to her suggestions of strangling Alfred Blatt, castrating Joseph, or plotting the death of my mother.

"I will not," I would scream above her commanding voice, and she would vanish, staring into an empty paperweight, or plotting false fates and artificial murders.

Dr. Phalatrope was not content with this means of control; he wanted me to find a permanent solution to Madelaine.

"I cannot tell you the answer, but I can tell you to search," he answered ambiguously when I begged him to tell me how to proceed.

Mrs. Gilligan is always Mrs. Gilligan no matter how I see her. Yet this knowledge does not help. I thought Madelaine was gone forever, but the moment I began to trust Joseph she returned. Why do I need her to defend me? The trial is making no progress. My treatment is static. I am being tried for the wrong crime. I miss Gerard; my asthmatic attacks have increased since he left. Much of the time I can hardly breathe. Dr. Phalatrope asks if I want to see my husband. My husband made me into a prop inseparable from himself I tell Dr. Phalatrope, who says it was partly my fault and might be worked out. He overestimates my strength. Half the time I think that my husband is dead. Sometimes I forget that he exists. Dr. Phalatrope thinks I should deal with my feelings more directly, but I cannot. He has also told me that my husband is trying to change and has thrown away many of the erotic costumes he designed for me. However, I myself am enslaved to them, and this news does not make me happy. I have decided that I do not want to see my husband. It is an arbitrary decision, but I have no feeling for him. I don't care if he changes or doesn't change; it has nothing to do with me. I have begun to talk to the woman with the pansies. She answers when she can. I no longer call her mother. Sometimes I forget.

I became weary of the trial. In fact I saw no reason to listen to the testimonies. Only I knew the truth. But this attitude annoyed Joseph, who was trying to protect me.

"If you are not interested in your own defense, then you might as well change the plea to guilty, and that will be the end of it," he said angrily.

"But I am interested in my own defense," I said.

The problem was that I saw all possibilities. I knew that my moments of indifference were dangerous. Madelaine was ever-watchful and would take possession of me at these times.

Most terrifying of all were the increasingly frequent occurrences of blankness. When Florence was called as a witness for the defense, I felt something agonizing within me like a terrible memory. Was it a nightmare I'd had long ago? Something has happened to her, a husband was involved, I thought. Yet I could not identify Florence or my relationship to her. What has happened, I wondered with alarm, knowing that there had been a strong bond between us.

"The defendant has stated on several occasions that you were a teacher in the same school as she was. Is this true?" asked Alfred Blatt.

It is all a mistake, a preposterous error, I wanted to shout. But I was silent.

"No," said Florence, lapsing into some dream that I could not enter. With a feeling of disorientation and horror, I realized that whatever hallucinations tormented Florence—they had nothing to do with me.

Pale and withdrawn, she could not focus upon the questions that were being asked.

"Do you know the deceased?" Alfred continued.

Florence laughed and then lapsed into silence.

"Florence may step down," said Judge Phalatrope.

Evenings I listened to her weeping; I watched from afar as she rocked an imaginary baby in her arms and smiled.

"I have never known her," I told Dr. Phalatrope. "Yet I have the feeling that we shared many things together. I must be insane." I burst into deep lonely sobbing.

"Sometimes," said Dr. Phalatrope, "people try to share fantasies.

And when the fantasy loses its grip or purpose they have no means of communication."

"Do you mean the people here?" I asked.

"It is not so different outside," he said.

I looked at him for a moment. "Have you shared my fantasies?" I asked him. He did not answer, but I thought of him laughing with Mrs. Gilligan, or watching over Florence's imaginary labor. "You must be very tired," I said.

"Yes, I have been lost many times and driven you further away. I have been entrenched in your fantasies. You see, I believe that people must live through their fantasies until they work themselves out of them alone. If I abort a fantasy, something of value, a great clue, is lost forever."

"And when will I be free?"

He looked very sad. "No one is ever free," he said. "But to be able to move back and forth from world to world without too much injury is a good sign. Don't be too anxious. It is not necessary to push too fast."

He left me, to see someone else or to think or dream, the dreams and fantasies of an ordinary man.

I am not happy to live in an empty world, without Florence, Gerard, or Hannah. I find reality empty, purposeless, and more painful than my vilest nightmares. I know no one. I feel completely isolated. It is worse than insanity. Or is this true insanity?

I slept a dreamless sleep, empty of vision or fear or desire. And I awoke with the feeling that my life was ending. But Madelaine is still here, I reassured myself with a mixture of fear and relief. I have only to summon her.

PART THREE

THE END OF THE TRIAL

The trial gradually dissipated—not that it didn't continue. But no one adhered to the rules any longer. Everyone spoke out of turn, clapping or hissing as their mood dictated. Even the judge no longer sat on his imperial chair or wore his crown.

"There is no defendant," I said, with authority. "I am Madelaine."

The jurors, who were scattered about the room sleeping or chatting, stamped their tin feet in disapproval.

"You are Elaine the murderer," said Mrs. Gilligan as Hannah applauded.

"I am Madelaine, who only plots and dreams of murder. There is no Elaine."

"She has escaped. Let me find her," said Alfred, starting up the staircase.

"You will not find her there, Alfred," said Dr. Phalatrope.

"You must be hiding her then," accused the D.A.

"Where is she?" demanded the jurors, coming to life in unison.

"She has vanished for the time being. I suggest you proceed with things as they are," suggested the judge.

Alfred looked perplexed.

"Perhaps Alfred has murdered her," said Joseph.

"Nonsense," said Madelaine. "They are both dead by choice."

"I quite agree," said the judge.

"In that case, I am not the defense attorney, having no one to defend," whined Joseph, covering his face.

"Who are you?" I asked.

Joseph did not answer.

"There are some possibilities," he finally said weakly. "Florence's brother . . . or the husband of the missing defendant, a gynecologist . . ."

Mrs. Gilligan laughed.

"You may not laugh at Joseph just because he is no one," I said, wheezing. "Who are you?"

"I am not sure," said Mrs. Gilligan, chewing her rock candies nervously.

"It takes some courage," said the judge, "to admit to not knowing who you are. It's a starting point."

"The trial is finished," I said. (Madelaine, gasping for breath, was silent.) "Elaine confesses to the murder of herself."

"Case closed," said Judge Phalatrope, and everyone applauded or collapsed.

———

"Since I am Madelaine, you cannot intimidate me any longer," I told my husband, who hung over the examining table.

"Elaine, be reasonable," he said, putting on his rubber gloves. "You know you need me to protect you from the world."

"Elaine is dead. I, Madelaine, need no protection; in fact I have plotted your death in one hundred ways."

"That is not so unusual under the circumstances," he said. But I noticed the trembling of his rubber hands.

"Are you sure you won't lie down on the table?" he asked without looking at me.

I laughed my husky laugh and sent flashes of light from my snake into his eyes.

"I think I have a right to know why you won't let me examine you," he said. "You always used to," he added mournfully.

"I didn't realize I could refuse," I said, watching him remove his gloves and toss them on the floor in despair.

Sadly, his eyes full of tears, he put his instruments into a black case.

"You did your best," I said.

"Do you really believe that?" asked Dr. Phalatrope.

"I suppose so; what else is there to believe?"

He was about to say something when Alfred Blatt came running over to the formica-topped table at which we sat. "Someone has taken my nail file," he whined helplessly.

"I think you just misplaced it," said Dr. Phalatrope.

"People are always taking my things," he said, but he went off to look for it.

"Everyone does the best he can," I said absently, thinking of the gold ring that Dr. Phalatrope kept in his vest pocket.

———

At night my husband knocked. He tiptoed around the room, scrutinizing everything. He searched my drawers for the gold ring. Then he wept quietly in the chair beside my bed.

"I want one more chance," he whispered.

"It is impossible," I told Dr. Phalatrope. "He doesn't realize that Elaine is dead and cannot come back."

But Sir Phalatrope knew that despite my protestations she was present a good deal of the time. I ignored her thoughts and opinions as being inappropriate.

"Why have you murdered her?" he asked again and again.

"I realize that she committed no external crimes. However she is guilty of existing."

"You are trying to say that her existence is a failure as far as you are concerned."

"I have always suspected that. It is part of the reason for her death."

That night I put the chair against the door to bar my husband's entrance.

"I made you feel like a failure," he said, puffing his pipe, his chair bent back at a dangerous angle.

"Sit straight in your chair," I said in a harsh voice. He hesitated and then straightened the chair so it was flat on the floor.

"I'm sorry I made you feel like a failure," he said, puffing.

"No pipe puffing in my room," I commanded calmly.

Obediently he put the pipe away from his mouth and soon it went out.

"It's nice of you to speak to me this evening. I know I was critical and demanding in bed."

"Nonsense," I said, realizing something for the first time. "I murdered myself long before I met you. You had nothing to do with it. Do whatever you please."

"That's unfair," he said, rising and coming toward me.

"Stay where you are," I said. He sat down again.

"You know I made you unhappy. I picked on you, examined you, reprimanded and silenced you. At least let me take the blame."

"If it comforts you then take it, but you could not have treated me that way without my co-operation."

"I destroyed you," he said.

"You had very little to do with it," I shouted after him.

And then very slowly he melted until there was a pool of liquid wax on the chair. Magically the wax dissolved, leaving the room full of smoke.

———

Dr. Phalatrope came running. He banged at the door. I opened it, gasping for air. He picked up the pipe whose last spark had begun to smoke in the waste basket.

"Whose pipe is this?" he asked.

"My husband's," I answered mockingly. "Do you think that keeping the gold ring in your vest pocket is sufficient to keep him out of this room?"

Quickly he threw water in the waste basket and opened the windows—false windows that looked at silver space.

"Who left the pipe here?" he asked again.

"My husband," I answered, laughing.

THE BOX

I persuaded Joseph to make a handsome ebony box three feet long and two feet wide.

At first he insisted upon an explanation, so I told him that one would be forthcoming. Feeling somewhat ridiculous, he carefully measured, nailed, and sanded it. At my direction he added a top which had handsome brass hinges on one side and a lock on the other. Finally he became infatuated with the beauty of the object that he had created; he no longer demanded a purpose. (Dr. Phalatrope watched this work proceeding, thinking hard and stroking his beard.) Last I asked him to line the inside with green velvet. He was reluctant to do this, having fallen in love with the starkness of it, but he could refuse me nothing. What a magnificent box, stained to perfection, gently glossed, catching every gleam of light and transforming it, smelling of fresh wet trees.

I brought it into my room. Inside I placed the gold ring that I had reclaimed from the bewildered Dr. Phalatrope. It gleamed on the dark velvet. Next to the ring I placed an erotic manual and a teaching manual as well as a hexagonal eye mask that lay hidden in the second drawer of my night table.

There are so many things that belong inside, I thought, remembering certain sponge, silver, and silken apparitions. However, I decided to exclude these.

"It is my coffin," I informed Joseph, who watched my operation curiously.

"I will have no part in this morbidity," he said. But I had discovered that people did not mean such things.

"You are an essential part and I need your help," I said, kissing him. He began to laugh. I observed this suspiciously, since I had never seen Joseph laughing.

"It is much too small for you. You've made an error in your calculation. Just try to get inside it."

"I've made no mistake. It is a much younger Elaine that is to be buried. I want as much as possible to be destroyed."

"Of what?" he asked.

"Of time on earth—of past time on earth."

"In that case the box is too big."

"It is not meant for a baby but for a child, a child who has already experienced enough of life. It is exactly the right size."

———

In the starless night we went silently down the spiraling stairs to the unfinished basement below. It was dank and alive with the sounds of rats and mice scurrying back and forth inside the walls, or the frantic exit of one who was desperately searching for food.

"Here," I said, indicating an area of floor in front of some moth-eaten black drapes. Fortunately the floorboards were old and easy to remove. It took less than an hour for three of them to be lifted out with the help of Joseph's tools.

"What if Dr. Phalatrope hears noise and comes downstairs?" he whispered anxiously.

We did not guess that on a top step the magician sat silently, watching the ceremony, scarcely daring to breathe.

A stench of wet decay came from beneath the floorboards. And there amidst the skeletons of starving rats we lowered the beautiful coffin bearing the body of Elaine.

After the floorboards were nailed into place with a muffled rubber-heeled hammer, we said in unison, "May she rest in peace."

Then we sang the dirge which I had prepared for my funeral.

Who clipped your wings
My child my child?
Who clipped your wings
Before you could fly?
Who put the pinpoints
Into your lovely eyes
Who took the sun from your view.

Who with his knife
Tore out your tongue
Before you could laugh or cry?
Who   my child?
Who   my child?

Was it you   yourself?
Was it you
Who clipped your wings
Who put the pinpoints in your eyes?

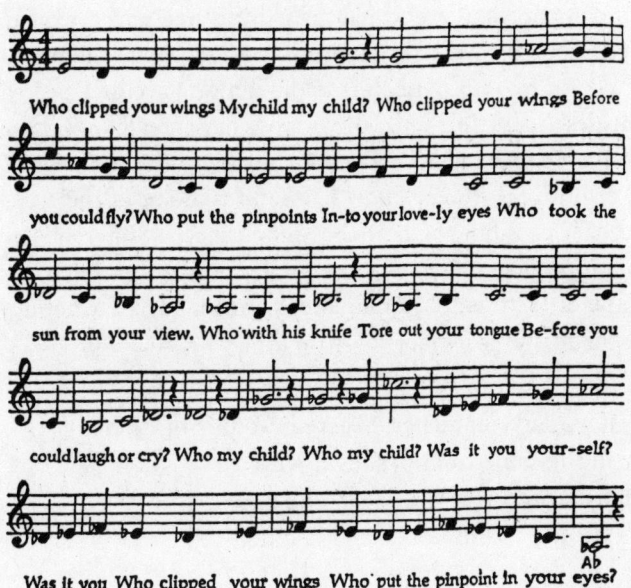

Who clipped your wings My child my child? Who clipped your wings Before

you could fly? Who put the pinpoints In-to your love-ly eyes Who took the

sun from your view. Who with his knife Tore out your tongue Be-fore you

could laugh or cry? Who my child? Who my child? Was it you your-self?

Was it you Who clipped your wings Who put the pinpoint in your eyes?

"You are using me as a tool for your creations," complained Joseph when the sacred rites were over.

I laughed merrily. "Isn't that how it should be after all this time? And I thought you hadn't noticed."

"It is only because I love you," he said.

"It has not a thing to do with love," I protested, with superior wisdom.

———

During the weeks that followed my funeral, I felt a sense of contentment. My husband understood the situation and did not persist in his attempts at a reconciliation. Nor did he visit me at night. It was Joseph who sat at the foot of my bed smoking a pipe he had carved until I fell asleep.

Joseph follows me through the days. We plant seeds, play checkers and dominoes, carve crude bowls from which we eat, despite the puzzled or hostile looks that surround us. Often we play with wooden figurines that he has carved and I have painted; they are a man called No one and a woman called Nobody. We write and enact plays about them, but more often we improvise. It is as though we have dropped all identities that society and our fantasies have created. We have become No one and Nobody who are childlike, spontaneous, and primitive. I do not know if Joseph is aware of their significance; possibly for him the significance is different. Dr. Phalatrope does not interfere, but I can tell that he is not completely satisfied. I suppose he is waiting for a further development, but we are happy with things the way they are.

"Shall we sail somewhere?" asked No one of Nobody.

"It's all the same to me," she answered.

"Where would you like to go?" he asked.

"You decide," said Nobody. "I decided yesterday."

"I can't think of anyplace to go," he said.

"Perhaps there is someplace we will find on the way."

"I warn you that the sea is rough," No one said hesitantly.

"I know all about the dangers of the sea. Let's sail anyway."

"I see an island of flowers," shouted No one.

"You are having visions. I see nothing," said Nobody.

"Why set sail each day," asked No one, "if you find nothing?" He was angry and started turning the small craft around.

"I can't think of anything else to do," she answered.

"Tomorrow you can stay ashore and I will go alone. I can find islands of flowers."

"You can only find false things," said Nobody.

"It's better than nothing," he answered.

"Perhaps it is, but I can't find them."

"What if I find something real?" said No one with excitement.

"Ho, ho, ho," laughed Nobody. "You know you can't."

No one got mad and threw her overboard.

Alfred Blatt steals the figurines when we are not looking. I find them beneath the table at which he sits and files his nails. Laughing, I crawl beneath and retrieve them. He storms and bangs his feet. In a rage he throws his nail file across the corridor and then anxiously searches for it. He cries quite often because he used up his peach nail polish and had to settle for a rose shade which he despises. I think he cries because Hannah has disappeared. He claims that he is being deceived and abused. Someone has given him a wig on a styrofoam head which he styles and restyles. None of the patients will let him give them pedicures or set their hair because he becomes frustrated with the result and pulls it very hard or messes it up in a frenzy. The other day he removed the wig from the false head and put it on his own head. He sleeps with it and is always looking into mirrors.

"Does the burial of Elaine solve all your problems?" asked Dr. Phalatrope.

"Yes, I am happier since the funeral," I answered. "And what objection do you have?"

"I don't think you have made any progress with Madelaine," he answered.

"She has gone away for now and I am content to be Nobody."

"But you keep her in reserve?"

"Of course I do, since I must. That's a ridiculous question to ask."

"Am I boring you?"

"I would say so," I answered. (Oh, what has happened to the magician?)

"Yes . . . you and Joseph are quite absorbed these days. Just try to give some thought to Elaine."

"Don't mention her," I answered, dashing out of my room and leaving poor Dr. Phalatrope alone.

———

"He understands nothing," I whispered to Joseph who was whittling a small pipe for No one.

"You mean he doesn't understand that Elaine is dead forever."

"Don't go jumping to conclusions," I warned him.

"I made a pipe for No one and a bed for . . ."

"It's a nice bed. Tell me who it's for," I said.

"I'm not sure," he answered.

"What a fool you are, making a bed and not knowing who it's for," I said.

Joseph looked hurt. "I thought they could decide about the bed," he said.

Mrs. Gilligan was watching and laughing. "The children are at play again," she said.

"Keep your opinions to yourself, Madelaine Gilligan," I said sternly. She continued laughing, but said no more.

"Whose bed is this?" asked Nobody, who was all dressed up in her crescent dress.

"It's mine," said No one in a weak voice.

"I see, and you've given no thought to where I will sleep."

"It's big enough for two," said No one, moving over.

"So that's what it's all about. I can't even have my own bed."

"If you like, I'll make you one," he answered, disappointed.

"Where do I sleep tonight while you are making my bed. Why isn't that my bed?" asked Nobody, getting angry.

"You can have it," said No one, getting out of bed almost in tears.

"So it really makes no difference to you one way or the other," said Nobody, getting hysterical.

"What do you want?" asked No one, falling on the floor in despair.

"I want you to want something," answered Nobody, weeping.

"But you don't let me."

"That's a lie," she said. "You have to want something badly enough to stick to it, even if I disagree."

"You're impossible, you know I can't want anything that badly. In fact it's hard for me to want anything at all."

"You'll have to," said Nobody resolutely.

"You mean you won't decide who is sleeping where?" he asked.

"I'll decide when your decision is strong enough. Otherwise there is nothing to decide about."

"We might be up all night and I still won't know," said No one.

"There's no hurry. I used to be like you, so I understand it," she added.

"You're always putting yourself above me," cried No one in a rage. "I'll sleep on the floor."

"No, I disagree," said Nobody. "You won't sleep on the floor. That's wrong."

"I thought it was what you really wanted."

"I told you not to make your decision by what you think I want. It's just as likely to be wrong anyhow."

"You confuse me deliberately," accused No one.

"I do not. I can't help it if I'm more decisive than you. I used to be like you," said Nobody.

Joseph threw Nobody and No one across the floor. "I'm tired of that lying. What makes you think you've changed so much?"

"I never said I changed," I told Joseph before going into my room.

I have triumphed over Joseph, as usual, I thought.

"But not over me," she said, stepping forth from behind the maroon drapes. I was alarmed; I had not called her and I did not need her yet.

Madelaine moved closer to me, grinning with the false smile I knew so well, her large bosom heaving under its tight black taffeta shroud.

"What do you want?" I asked, cowering in a corner of my bed.

"I will not be part of you any more," she said. "I have had enough."

"And who are you to decide such things?" I asked, surprised at my daring. "It is I who decide your comings and goings."

"But you haven't decided," she said, pacing about the room, the taffeta slips sparking from rapid friction. "You cannot have it both ways."

"I'll have it any way I choose—three ways if I like."

"No you won't; you've overestimated my flexibility. I am worn out from being pushed back somewhere and then suddenly having to find my way outside."

"You are wrong. I never buried you. It was Elaine whose funeral I officiated over."

"At least you know where she stands. But I have become vague. Either I take over completely, and now is a perfect time, since Elaine is dead, or I disappear completely."

"You mustn't disappear—not yet; I need time to decide and think," I pleaded.

"You cannot be Nobody forever. There is no more time. You think that you control me—well I'll prove that to be an illusion. I'll give you twenty-four hours from now to make up your mind."

"How dare you threaten me and give me time spans," I said weakly and half to myself. Madelaine was gone—Madelaine of my dreams of the death that clung to me since I first realized the power she had over my imagination and will. But how could I live without Madelaine?

Reality is gray, leafed with snow—snow turning to deep brownish pools without bottom—cold voids, silence everywhere. Phantoms hover overhead, emitting a stench of putrefaction, swooping downward and then curtaining themselves like grotesque dagger-beaked birds. They can come to no conclusions. It is a frozen hand that grasps the edge of the pool while birds peck at its fingers and then disappear behind a velvet cloud. Reality is the death of dreams, the gradual seeping away of energy—green banging hard for a moment and then reappearing as ash. Dreams end with fantasies. There is only displaced pain and constant ticking. For they have measured it by time. One must watch each cold day disappear with measured beats—faster, faster, though you may run and cry against it, hands soaked with blood, bones stiff, overcalcified, mouth gaping from hunger and eyes, unblinking against the savage light. Reality—no masks, no erotic symbols, illusions, false dreams of love or success. It is too heavy a burden after the nights of corrupt ecstasy, the broken pledges, the sense of purpose however absurd, debasing, or sentimental. Now there is no sense of purpose, no eyes that one can meet without seeing the coldness and indifference within. One who wakes from the dead can no longer be deceived. Then how to roam this land where all is false, changing, dead and ready to grab and throw away at the same second. Is there nothing to do but march in this frozen country, blades of light destroying your eyes. The hands of corpses seem to hold yours but let go the moment the danger of the cold pool is near. To march to the boring hostile rhythm of clocks, to wake to the sameness of the sun—to hope for nothing. I am the dead walking. I recognize no one for they were all my creations. And no longer able to create I must see. Not to see black or white but perpetual gray—the gray of cruelty, the gray of destruction, of love, the gray of survival, the gray of reality. My husband is part of the gray—the personality he sought to impose upon me, his perfectionism, the erotic games he taught me—all part of flat gray. Where do I go now? Back to his home, his erratic solicitude, his clocked moments of love and kindness, against a background of icy death? Or do I wander forever—filling up that endless ticking with work or pain? On and on I march, meeting jaded eyes all over, eyes of death, of false hope, laughing mouths, artificial frolicking over ice-glazed swamps. I would rather stay here, where veils still give me some respite from the clear light and mutilated faces outside. Yes, I have reclaimed my own fantasies and returned the identities I had fused with or stolen—except for one. I will miss the color of my madness. The image of the powerful magician has gone. Time, even here, is ticked off into my ear second by second, minute by minute until I scream.

"Dr. Phalatrope," I said, "I need Madelaine, but I don't need her all the time . . . yet I am afraid to live without her. You must think of something quickly."

He was silent for a long time. "If you are so afraid of Madelaine, why can't you let her go forever?"

"You know that answer," I said angrily. "She protects me from . . . from something—I don't even know what. Please let her stay for a while."

"So, when you want to demand something, you would like Madelaine to take the responsibility."

"Yes, yes. Elaine is dead anyhow."

"And you let your husband bury her again. How clever you are," he said.

"I buried her myself. He just helped," I protested.

"If that is your choice, then you have made the decision already. Why did you bother coming to me? Madelaine will be here to stay."

"You don't care, do you, you old fraud?"

"If you don't care, no one else will," he answered calmly.

"I don't understand you. How can you be so indifferent to what happens to me? I'll strike you."

"You mean Madelaine will strike me, don't you?"

"No, I don't. I will strike you myself. Do you think I can't even strike you, without Madelaine?"

"That's what you've been telling me."

"Well I hate you enough to strike you myself."

"But you are dead and buried. How can that be?"

"Nonsense. Don't tell me you believe that I am in that coffin. It is empty. I swear it is empty. Ask Joseph. No, don't ask Joseph. He thinks I am dead."

"Whom are you trying to fool?"

"You know very well I am not in that box. I am right here," I said, clenching my fists.

"Then dig up the box and prove it," he said.

"I will not. I will certainly not do that."

"All right, you can stay here forever, Madelaine."

"I am not Madelaine. I am not Madelaine."

"That is for you to decide," he said.

THE APPOINTED HOUR

———————

She came at the appointed hour. All day I had waited in my room, refusing to see Joseph, who knocked at my door begging me to play Nobody and No one with him.

"I have finished with that game," I said curtly as he sobbed outside. Dr. Phalatrope led him away. I heard him muttering to Joseph about changes, endings and transformations; I am not certain. Perhaps he became Nobody and sailed the unpredictable waters with No one.

"Are you sure you don't want to see me?" asked Dr. Phalatrope outside the locked door.

"I want to meet Madelaine alone."

———

With confidence, but looking a bit fatigued, she stepped from behind the maroon drapes. She said nothing, but stared at me, her gray eyes glittering in the light of the metallic lamp. Leaves crackled on her shoulders—dead brown, others streaked with purples and odd greens.

"Leaves are falling on the white horse; it's time for our journey," whispered the magician.

Madelaine shivered as a blast of air came from the window, causing the maroon drapes to move behind her. Bat-like she spread her arms to keep the leaves outside, to stop the wild horse who snorted and reared behind her.

"The white horse is you needn't ever step outside waiting to hurt and silence you try again come to me forever to exist despite surrender forever the uncertain never ticking gray sunlight come break the coffin into my arms veiled trees are promising something uncertain beware forever I will crush her you need me try to protect me from the light go beyond the phantom silencers me me always to find where the magician is it's dangerous and an illusion happiness disguised clicking screaming predators of day as an ordinary man." (They spoke at once.)

I watched her writhing, gyrating, drowning in images of men she tantalized with net-like masks and feathered whips who disappeared like dust of leaves. "My disguises are endless," she said. "Without them you are lost." I promise you pain said the magician inside as she trembled not knowing whether to surrender or advance. Endless desert, abandoned birds, no water under rocks, a few flowers—the world like a heartbeat or a clocktick with uncertain stalling and stopping and jumping—in all a spectacle for the strong or wise. Decide. "I'm smothering in this taffeta shroud. It's safe. The leaves are also nice, let them in." Sweeping in, sweeping out, a disarray of sequined stirrups, tantalizing manuals glowing with precise rules and excessive penalties; everything was summoned and displayed in desperate fury. Entwined with bristly ropes she danced and beat the hearts of trees with silver bars. Faster and faster she wound tin men and torched mute mannequins to pools of wax. Hot images recreated themselves and exploded in endless repetition. I summoned every bit of strength to keep them living, moving, blinding her with snakebelly crawling and sudden upward lunging. She wheezed and gasped until her own electric apparition sent bits of black taffeta burning to needles of stenched smoke. The horse moaned as flesh shivered with blasts of air and drafts of light, and bones slumped finally quietly on plain veined leaves.

—

Fear and the timerock of one pumping heart. "I am naked."

ABOUT THE AUTHOR

ELAINE KRAF (1936–2013) was a writer and painter. She was the author of four published works of fiction: *I Am Clarence* (1969), *The House of Madelaine* (1971), *Find Him!* (1977), and *The Princess of 72nd Street* (1979)—as well as several unpublished novels, plays, and poetry collections. She was the recipient of two National Endowment for the Arts awards, a 1971 fellowship at the Bread Loaf Writers' Conference, and a 1977 residency at Yaddo. She was born and lived in New York City.

ABOUT THE TYPE

The principal text of this Modern Library edition was set in a digitized version of Janson, a typeface that dates from about 1690 and was cut by Nicholas Kis (1650–1702), a Hungarian working in Amsterdam. The original matrices have survived and are held by the Stempel foundry in Germany. Hermann Zapf (1918–2015) redesigned some of the weights and sizes for Stempel, basing his revisions on the original design.